ABOUT LEVY

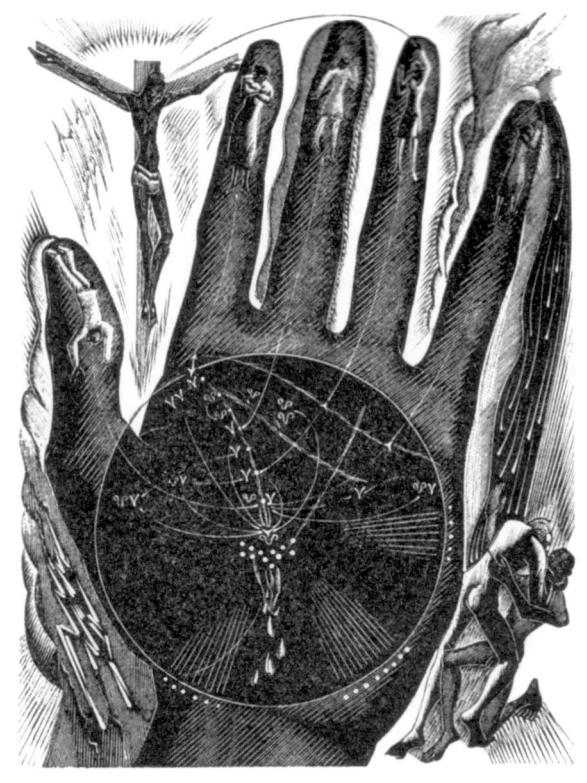

Our authorised representative in the EU for product safety is
Easy Access System Europe, Mustamäe tee 50, 10621 Tallinn, Estonia
gpsr.requests@easproject.com

About Levy

ARTHUR CALDER-MARSHALL

This edition first published in 2015
by Faber & Faber Ltd
Bloomsbury House, 74–77 Great Russell Street
London WC1B 3DA
First published in 1933

Printed by Books on Demand GmbH, Norderstedt

All rights reserved
© The Estate of Arthur Calder-Marshall, 2015

Frontispiece by Blair Hughes-Stanton

The right of Arthur Calder-Marshall to be identified
as author of this work has been asserted in accordance
with Section 77 of the Copyright, Designs and Patents Act 1988

This book is sold subject to the condition that it shall not, by way of
trade or otherwise, be lent, resold, hired out or otherwise circulated
without the publisher's prior consent in any form of binding or cover other than
that in which it is published and without a similar condition including this
condition being imposed on the subsequent purchaser

A CIP record for this book is available from the British Library

ISBN 978–0–571–32448–4

'What a piece of work is a man! How noble in reason! how infinite in faculty! in form and moving, how express and admirable! in action, how like an angel! in apprehension, how like a god! the beauty of the world! the paragon of animals!'

Hamlet, Act II, Scene 2.

ABOUT LEVY

1.   'You don't know,' the new man said, who had a fawn coat slung on his arm. His teeth, stuck astraggle in his jaw, clicked on the glass. When his arm fell like a signal over the bar, the counter rapped, the beer jumped nearly to the rim. Then it slobbered back to its level. 'You don't know. I know. But you don't know.'

'And who are you?' Jelliff said. He was a stout man, whose mouth burst in his face, an over-ripe tomato. 'You to know?'

'Aye, who's 'e to know?' the others muttered, sucking clays and cobs. One spat a bomb of dottle, which splayed the sawdust. He dragged his foot over the boards and smeared it out with his boot.

'Sankey,' the new man said, raising his glass again while they thought over his name. He sat on the high stool, his neck stretched to the glass and pulsing with beer.

They took the name in and spat it out to each other in turn, like feeding fish.

'Sankey,' Jelliff said. 'That's why you know; 'cos

ABOUT LEVY

your name's Sankey. Not by any chance the Judge himself?'

'The Judge! The Judge!' Sankey said.

'No relation of the Judge?' Jelliff said.

The new man swiped his lips with his hand. 'There *are* other Sankeys.'

'That's why you know, is it?' Jelliff said. ''Cos your name's Sankey, and y'er no relation of the Judge.'

'I *know*,' said the new man. 'I know, because I've travelled. I've been places you've never heard of; I've known people all the world over, and I've seen things happen you couldn't believe, not in sleep even. What d'you do? Just stay swilling. Then what do you know? Seeing the world through the bottom of a glass. Old and mild, old and mild. What do you know but old and mild? It's what you all are, old and mild.'

'I was in France,' Jelliff said, 'during the war.'

'Join the Army,' Sankey said, 'and see the world. Travel in the ranks with pocket-money from the King. What do they see? Rotten death and low-down places. I know. I was in France, too, during that war. But any fool can see low-down places. I'm telling you. That's not life, that's not fun.'

A man spoke from the corner by the partition, dirty fellow, builder's foreman, lived No. 6 Grape Street, married, with five children. He hadn't said a word; now he spoke out.

'What's fun?' he said. 'What d'you call fun?'

ABOUT LEVY

'He knows,' Sankey said. 'Levy knows what fun is.'

The heads swung back to Sankey; the bent shoulders lurched in his direction. Their mouths were twisted; the teeth showed broken and yellow between lips.

Sankey leant back on his stool, holding himself up away from them with an elbow on counter.

'Leevy?' Clarrie said, wiping a mug with his cloth. 'You heard the latest about him?'

'No. 'Ve they let 'im off?' Sankey said quickly.

'I don't know that; I mean the story they tell,' he said, leaning across the counter, and spoke in a whisper this, 'What did Edith say when Leevy knocked on her bedroom door?'

'Aw, I've heard that,' a fellow said, and spat.

'Go on,' Jelliff said, 'we haven't heard it.'

'Go on,' they said, craning forward. Some bent their ears to catch it.

'Leevy things in the hall,' Clarrie said and recoiled, polishing the mug sharply between thumb and forefinger.

They just roared, crumpled the air with cries from heaving lungs. And laughed and coughed till they wept.

Clarrie leaned forward.

'Leave ye things in the hall,' he said. Then he took another glass, dipped it in the steaming basin, sluiced it, shook it. He stood back laughing till he had to stop polishing to wipe the tears from his eyes.

ABOUT LEVY

They all laughed and drank up their glasses and had another one. It was getting on to closing time.

'What'll you have, Clarrie?' Jelliff said.

'Mine's a mild,' Clarrie said, setting the mug down and going to the pump.

'That was a good one of yours,' Jelliff said. 'How does it go?'

'Leevy things in the hall,' Clarrie said, raising his glass. 'All the best.'

'Happy days,' Jelliff said, and blew froth to the floor.

The new man hadn't spoken while they were laughing; had just sat glum, watching.

Now he said, 'Levy knows what's fun.'

'Well, tell us what's fun, then,' said the dirty builder. 'You know. You've travelled.'

'Power,' the new man said, 'power's what's fun. Some've got it in the arm, in the body. Carnera's got it in the arm; I've got it in the arm. Feel my biceps.'

He bared and crooked his arm.

Jelliff felt his biceps.

'Like whipcord,' Sankey said. 'Like iron bars. I can break chains with them. I bind them,' and he crooked his arm, 'and snap them. How old 'ld you think I was?'

'Old as lying,' Jelliff said.

'Fifty,' the foreman said.

'Sixty-seven, I'm telling you. That's what I am. Do I look sixty-seven?'

'No, just ugly,' a low voice said.

ABOUT LEVY

Sankey got up from his stool. He was a tall man, full of beer. 'Who said that?'

They sat round beneath him looking from one to another.

'Eighteen-sixty-five, Feb. fifteen, was the happy day. And it's exercises. I've got me weak spots; who hasn't? But I know them. How many of you know yours?'

'Last orders, gentlemen, please.'

'Some 've got it in the arms,' he went on. 'Some 've got it in the mind. Levy'd got it in the mind. Killed that man, he did. I know. I've travelled. Killed him with his mind. He's a real man; alive, Levy is.'

'What do you mean?' The foreman, puzzled, came over to him. The others were talking and getting last-minute drinks.

A bell clattered. 'Last orders.'

'I mean,' Sankey said, 'just look at them. They're not men; sheep, dungy sheep.'

'Who 're you calling dungy sheep?' Jelliff said.

'You,' Sankey said. 'God spew you. Levy could kill his man. But you're just a sheep, sweetbreads.'

Jelliff couldn't answer. He was getting his last glass before time. Then he said over shoulder, 'God spew me, eh?'

'Time, gentlemen, please. Time, please.'

' "God spew you," I said, from cellar to cess, where you belong.'

The bell clattered.

'Is there going to be a fight?' the foreman said.

ABOUT LEVY

'You bet there is,' the new man said.

Jack came up. He had the strength of a gorilla, and said, 'Hurry along, please,' jostling them.

Sankey was turned to the door by the press. The bell rang again. He looked round at Jelliff, who stooped to his drink like a dog.

'Right, I'm going,' he said, jerking his elbow into the foreman's ribs. 'I'm going, and don't push.'

2.   They sat upon the high seats, their gloves and papers on the bar.

'Well, here's,' the first said.

'Bung ho!' the second said.

'You knew him, you say?' the first said.

The second pushed back his bowler hat. 'You know him too. We've played rugger against him. You remember him: that little man who played for that hospital side.'

'Huh, little man, nippy, black-haired chap?'

'Nippy, yes, sir. Out with the ball before you knew where you were. Millar, despite his wing-forward business always being offside, never got him.'

'I remember him,' the first said; 'he tried blind side too much. When you knew that, you'd solved him.'

'Aren't you thinking of Bretzelbaum, the little man who played for the Old Paulines?'

'Yes, I am,' the first said. 'Good fellow, met him in Sandy's once; we were both awfully tight.'

'No, Levy, or however he says it, had a great

ABOUT LEVY

stunt of breaking away himself, and did it too. He was a slippery devil, and the way he started up his movements was a fair treat. Lovely pair of hands.'

'My God, I wish it was winter. There's nothing to play in summer.'

'Have another,' the second said. 'I belong to the Y.M.C.A. because of the games. They've got a gym. and damn fine baths.'

'They're not a bad lot of coves, are they? Yes, I will.'

'Good sports,' the second said. 'I said "bloody" in the baths there once, and nobody minded.'

'Those are the sort of people I like, broad-minded.'

'That's the scheme, and the Y.W.C.A. is just across the way; so your girl friend can have a bathe too.'

'O.K. baby,' the first said. 'And what do you think of Edith? A good-looking bird, eh?'

'Do me for a night or two,' the second said. 'But I'm surprised at Levy: he was a quiet chap. But the quiet ones, you know. Well, bung ho!'

'Here's to the quiet ones,' the second said, 'with knobs on.'

3.   Mrs. Bailey took the linen from the zinc bath, piece by piece, in her old hands, softened with soapy water. Raising her arm, she held up the flapping clothes against her face in the wind and pegged them to the rope. A fence of worn slats, of which some were snapped at the half, divided this plot from the next. The sky here was strewn with pulled cloud, the breeze quick on the sheets. Mrs. Handley came with her wash—she had her own trouble: the old man drank, had been out of work since the new road was finished; the last baby died, she said of hunger; she said there were too many mouths to fill, but people said she overlaid it when she saw it would always be a cripple—came with her wash hand-wrung, into the next plot and took down the prop. Then she walked to the fence, resting, as she was tired, her weight from her arm on the barked stick.

Mrs. Bailey looked back away from the rope.
'You're lucky,' Mrs. Handley said.
'What's wrong?'

ABOUT LEVY

'Your old man's dead. You've got the old age. What you wash is favour to folks; it's your own comfort.'

'I've washed for 'em these years; and why should I stop? I give it to you when it's too much for me alone.'

'I wash for me bare mouth's bread,' Mrs. Handley said. 'D'you think you'd see me do it, if I needn't to?'

Mrs. Bailey turned with a white shirt hanging down her body. 'You're young, girl, and strong,' she said. 'It's barely five years since you came in white to that house of yours, a bride.'

'Young! Five years! What older could I be, that have had four children since I came? Look at me torn arms, too.'

Mrs. Bailey dropped the shirt back with the rest and came to the fence.

'Five years,' she said. 'You call that a long time? You seen this Levy in the paper?'

'The man what poisoned another man? I've seen 'im.'

'Yes. Five years! A long time! Well, I nursed 'im; that was after Bailey died. I nursed him when he was a baby, and his mother before him. That's thirty years and more to set you thinking.'

'You nursed him?'

'When he was so small in his cradle till he was a big boy.'

'What was he like then?'

'A weakly thing. You've seen his picture in the

ABOUT LEVY

papers as he left the court, but his face was covered with his hand.'

'Yes, he was small and stooping as if falling forward,' the other said.

'I knew him better than his own mother and longer. Small and quiet he was always; no one knew what he was thinking. But not a minute's trouble, and he would come behind me and throw his arms round my neck as I was sitting mending of an afternoon. I was telling the new lady at the vicarage. I was sitting mending in one of their chairs which was bought in at the sale, and I remembered him coming up so quiet I didn't know he was there, and throwing his arms round my neck and kissing me.'

'They lived here, didn't they?'

'She did before she went off to marry one of them Jews, and she came back after he died because of Father Hill. She's buried behind the church there, but her stone's cracked now and fallen. Really that chair I sat in to-day was the child's by rights; Father Hill bought it in at the sale, and then he left it there. But it's old now and only good enough for me.'

'Was this Levy, who poisoned the other man, was he a queer kid?'

'When old Levy died, that was his father, he lay groaning nights, and the doctor came and gave him things to make him sleep: you know, when they're ill, they give them things to send them off and dull the pain. But he never went off quite, and I'd go in and sit with him, so that she could go and sleep.

ABOUT LEVY

Always at the end he had to have her holding his hand or he began crying and moaning terrible, like he was a bull fallen in a ditch. He couldn't see then; his eyes were swole up and he held my hand, thinking I was her, and cried, "Esther, Esther," which was her name. Once he cried, "Lay down beside me on the bed now; I want to feel your body against me, please." I'd heard him ask her and she wouldn't. His face was all swole, and she couldn't look at him; she couldn't bear it. So I squeezed his hand tight, and he grew quiet.'

'But the kid, was he queer?' the young woman said. 'Was he queer?'

'Bert said you wouldn't be able to tell the difference between him and anyone else. He said murderers were just ordinary, like you and me. But I said, "No, they're queer always. It's written in their hands."'

'I'm telling you,' Mrs. Bailey said, 'if you'll give me my time. He grew unnatural. The old man sort of recovered; he walked about, his head tied round in a cloth because it hurt his eyes to see, and his forehead was all scarred. And the boy, that's him who's in court this day, ran away from him and wouldn't stand to be touched by his own father. They who had been so fond before. And as for her, she couldn't even scarcely bear to undo the rag from his head, and had me in to dress him, him who had always been so independent. I reckon it was right in the end he should die, because they couldn't seem to do with him.'

ABOUT LEVY

'That's not a thing to say, Mrs. Bailey,' Mrs. Handley said. 'There's no one in this world so unwanted.'

'That's as may be. But when he passed away after six months of lingering,—I'm telling you I remembered it all as if it was yesterday as I was sitting in that there chair,—Miss Esther, that is, Mrs. Levy, she was dreadfully distressed; she carried on like a wild woman, and went to his grave,—every day at first,—with fresh blooms. The may was blowing when he died, and she went to the heath to fetch it. But Claude, the little one, wouldn't go with her after the first once, not to his own father's grave. I heard her ask him why he wouldn't come, and say it wasn't natural not to pay the dead their dues. But he just stood sulky and wouldn't answer, didn't give her back a word. Next time and ever after he hid when he knew she was coming for him.'

'He wouldn't go, not to his own father's grave?'

'Not to the churchyard where he was buried; not to the road even, which leads past the cemetery.'

'That was queer.'

'That was queer, but not the only queer thing I'm telling you. He was unnatural; she said he was unnatural. It kind of pained 'er he wouldn't pay dues to his dead father which was laying in the earth under those may blooms from the heath. Red may she plucked first, and laid it on the fresh soil. I saw with my own eyes, because I held the basket and gave it to her sprig by sprig, which she pressed in the ground. Later they turfed it, yer know: cut turf and spread it over. Then she says red wasn't very nice, not respectful enough, which was a sweet thought. As I sat in that chair sewing for the new lady, beautiful velvet curtains at fifteen and thruppence a yard, which makes me conjecture that she's got money of her own, Mrs. Handley, I saw in me mind's eye that little widow, her face so pale and drawn in her weeds, for she took his death sore, look up and say, "No, no, Susan. Red won't do; it's not respectful enough." So she got white may after that, and later peonies. All white flowers and the purple sort.'

'What was the other queer things he did?'

'Here are we gossiping, happy enough in spite of our little troubles.'

'Happy enough, I s'pose.'

'Here we are in our little gardens, I say to meself, talking while he's standing in the court on his trial for murder. Perhaps at this very moment the judge's his black cap on. Can you picture 'im, the judge in 'is black cap?'

'Bert said to me last night it might be one of us. It might as soon. It's all chance in the end.'

'Not might as soon be one of us. He was unnatural; there's no denying it. He was queer, to say the least. I was telling you. He seemed sort of happy when his father died. He didn't know

ABOUT LEVY

what it meant for his mother, what a blow it was to her. It happened sudden. He never spoke to her about his father, and he didn't answer when she told him to pray for him. Little Ruth, which was his sister, was so different, and clung to her mother's skirts and cried with 'er. She was such a help; while Master Claude stood sulky and sullen and didn't say a word, not a word of comfort to his poor mother, not an "I'm sorry, Mother, and I'll try and be a help": while little Miss Ruth was up and jolly with a "What can I do, Mother?" and "You must rest, Mother," and her little questions that brought tears to me eyes: "Is Daddy in God's bosom, Mother? Can he see us now?" I remember 'er answering simple and sweet, "Of course, dear, he can always see you, and he is blessing you now for being so good to your poor mother." I saw the boy's face puckered then like a dirty dishclout that's stiff with the washing-up. The next morning I went out in the sideyard to chop some wood for the new fires; the kitchener was alight then. I was helping, as there were no maids. When I came back with me arms bundled with kindling-wood, I saw smoke come from the door of the kitchen out in the scullery, right out through the back door even. I set down the kindling-wood quick as lightning on a chair, and I ran, yes, I was young then, into th' kitchen. What did I see?'

'What did you see, Mrs. Bailey?'

'You may well ask what I saw, Mrs. Handley.

ABOUT LEVY

There was smoke belching from that kitchener like a chimney stack. I couldn't see for the smoke at first. Then I saw in the grate a black thing smouldering half-burnt, which was her hat; a straw thing it was, and as I shook it to put it out, it sprung out all flames in me hand, and I had to douse it under the tap. Then I went back into the kitchen, choking with the fumes, and dug out the black stuff, which was smoking, with a little poker I had, sort of hooked at the end. It was stuffed right hard into the fire, and caught flame as I got it out bit by bit.'

'What was it, Mrs. Bailey?'

'That was her widow's dress, you see, which he had taken before she woke up; taken from her own room from the chair at her feet, tiptoeing as she lay abed.'

'He took it and burnt it?'

'And he owned up, too, as bold as bold; he wouldn't say why. Just kept saying he had. "Now punish me," he kept saying.'

'What did she do?'

'She beat 'im a treat, and docked his pocket-money for a year—he had sixpence a week that time—to help pay for the dress. But it wasn't that; it was the wilfulness of him pained her, with his father's body not cold in the house four weeks agone.'

'It was a mad thing,' Mrs. Handley said, 'mad and senseless for a lad to do.'

'It was mad and queer to see how he stayed so quiet and stubborn, till we thought that women-folk

ABOUT LEVY

weren't the people to rule 'im, which was part why Mrs. Levy came back here to live, to give the child over to Father Hill. He was a real man to humble the stubborn.'

'There, Mrs. Bailey. I told Bert this Levy was a queer one. Wasn't I right?'

'He was unnatural, Mrs. Handley, though I nursed him. As I told the new lady at the vicarage, I knew him better than his own mother.'

'Do you think he did it? Is he guilty?'

'Mrs. Handley, I say how should he be in court if he hadn't done something wrong? that's what I say.'

4.   'THE quad's strung with bunting.' Father Hill looked round from the window, hand raised, half-resting from the curtain, half-pushing it into the wall. 'It might be a regatta.'

Father Beasley lifted his thin body from the toes and then let it rest again, the heels on the fire-curb. 'Yes. The Head,' he said. 'He's begun decorating the place on Commemoration Day.'

'It's all right if it keeps fine,' the third priest said.

'Umph!' Beasley said, 'and yet again, Umph!'

Two ex-chaplains, Hill and Bubb, Beasley the present chaplain of Rockley, men of God, gods among boys. Hill now in a dock parish north; Bubb home from India on leave after dysentery, resting from the great work he is doing among the Hindus.

Bubb moved across; he was staying in the school, and wore a black cassock, girt with a smooth leather belt, gusseting from the thighs about lithe shanks. The two stood in the window peering down where parents moved across grass, pointing tongues of colour waving over them. They walked with

ABOUT LEVY

disconsolate ease and spoke in loud voices to show they were at home within the square of piled dormitories and common-rooms.

Beasley looked at the two. He had had to start again at the beginning: Bubb's mysticism had been absurd for boys; Hill ruled God out with a rod of iron. Their rough heads topped broad lumpy shoulders.

Then Hill turned and walked back, swinging his leg in a semicircle.

'Well,' he said, 'well. It's strange on Commemoration Day.'

He wore an ill-fitting clerical suit. Bubb knew what he meant; he came over too, grinning, who didn't want to.

As he said 'Tragic,' his mouth twitched.

Beasley walked over to the wireless and tried to get a station.

'I said our friend would come to a bad end,' Hill said, 'but I never thought my words would be so shockingly fulfilled.'

'Wasn't normal,' Bubb said.

Beasley stopped twisting knobs on his set, and said, 'Can't get anywhere this time of day, except Morse. Who's that you're speaking of?'

The two looked at each other. Father Hill swung a leg round, hand in pocket,—the leg bent like a wrought-iron figure's,—and flicked an ash into a pot of drooping flowers. He was an ex-boxing blue at Cambridge; he was at Pembroke. 'You've heard, of course. We were talking about Master Levy.'

ABOUT LEVY

'Who's he?'

'An O.R. among other things, who is on trial for murder.'

'Sounds rather unwholesome. I never read the papers.'

'He was under me,' Bubb said. His mouth twitched at the corners.

'I had high hopes of Master Levy when I adopted him,' Hill said. 'But he was a weakling. Had no guts.'

'The boys found that out,' Bubb said. 'They picked his weak spot and worried that. I did my best for him.'

'You know they're right,' Hill said. 'They've got an instinct for finding what's unhealthy in another lad and stamping on it.'

'I know,' Beasley said. 'The little beasts.'

'No, not little beasts. It hurts, of course, but so does cauterising.'

'You know, Beasley,' Bubb interrupted, 'because a thing hurts it doesn't mean it's bad. I see what Hill means: I've been in India, you see, and I'm a bit of a doctor. I've had to hurt people to cure them. The Indians are a wonderful people, of course, but they can't stand pain from a doctor.'

'We mustn't grow soft,' Hill said, lighting another cigarette from his stub.

'I did my best with the boy, you know,' Bubb went on. 'He was a difficult case. But when I saw him leading Common astray I had to talk seriously to him. He was such a nice kid, Andrew Common.'

ABOUT LEVY

'Common?' Father Hill said, 'I used to call him "Diddlums." '

'A nice kid,' Bubb said.

'Yes, "Diddlums" was what I called him. He was a beautiful hurdler. He'd 've got a boxing blue too, if he'd gone up. He really knew how to use his feet.'

'It was a beastly business,' Bubb said, 'but I always believe in nipping things in the bud. Prevention is better than cure.'

'I really took him because his mother asked me to on her deathbed. I'd been a father to them both after the real father died. Poor Esther Levy had no idea how to manage children.'

'Were there two?' Beasley said.

'Yes, a girl as well, called Ruth. But the father's people took her, and I don't know what happened to her. Sank back into orthodox Judaism, I suppose.'

'Do you believe he did it?' Bubb said.

'I'm afraid I do. I don't like to say it, but he's the type. It's not big men that commit that sort of murder; it's the little gutless men. And the motive, you can't get away from it.'

'The girl?'

'Yes, Edith Mason, or whatever her name is. If Claude had been a religious man, and not a professed atheist, I couldn't have prevented a suspicion. But as it is,' and he waved his hand, making the argument silently conclusive, 'you find with all these men who drift away from the Church that sex is at the bottom of it. They may have very high moral standards in

ABOUT LEVY

other ways. But in that one respect they seem to lose all scruples. I've seen it time and again.'

'That's fair enough,' Beasley said.

'And poison; if I'd been asked how he would commit a murder, I should have said poison without hesitation. He's half Jew and half Christian, with the scruples of neither. Just give the man the glass and watch him die before your eyes, then quietly clear out. That's his way.'

'But he didn't clear out.'

'The housekeeper came in a moment too soon.'

Beasley was looking out at the quad. 'The Bishop of Mahawaubi has arrived,' he said.

'It was a great scheme to get Bobby Rudlands to preach,' Hill said. 'To think that he's a bishop now. He was one of my best servers. He really looked beautiful in his red cassock; there's no other word. Captain of 'Varsity Rugger, half blue for running, captain of Keble cricket. "Big-hearted Bobby" they called him in Flanders.'

'Yet he was so small,' Bubb said. 'I remember him when he first came. He had bright, piercing eyes; very funny. It was only at the end he went wild.'

'Oh, Claude,' Hill said. 'I thought you meant Bobby Rudlands.'

The bugles flared.

'That means the procession in ten minutes' time,' Beasley said.

'There was talk of incense,' Hill said, 'wasn't there?'

ABOUT LEVY

'He used to come to my room for a little talk regularly every Thursday,' Bubb said. 'And of course to confessional.'

'Yes, but the Head wouldn't do it,' Beasley answered. 'He said the parents wouldn't stand for it.'

'As though that mattered,' Hill said.

5.   'THE other doctors in the hospital were nice to us, except old Bottle, of course; and he was different because, though he was a firebrand, everybody knew he had a heart of gold. The other doctors were always ready with their little joke—often even in the middle of a serious operation; they knew how to laugh. They treated us like the ladies we were, always well-spoken, yet never familiar. We worked hard in those days—such long hours standing; but I was young then. This happened long before my marriage. You see that picture on the piano; that's me in my uniform. There's a little shop in Brighton, the Western Road, where they take you cabinet ever so cheap the half-dozen. I was the prettiest girl in my ward by a long way. Which is saying no little, because Joyce was in my ward, who you met here last Whit-Monday and said was so nice looking. You didn't ought to have said that, George; you made me feel quite jealous, really you did. But if you'd said it at the time I'm speaking of, I shouldn't have felt jealous. I was the first girl always that they selected for

ABOUT LEVY

the flag-day; and most times I took more than anyone else, because I made all the doctors give to me before I went out to my post. All except this Levy. He was junior house surgeon, so that we couldn't help seeing a certain amount of each other. I never liked him. He was a Jew, but he wasn't coarse like most of the Jews you meet are. When he came to the hospital first he didn't have to shave; that'll show you for a dark-haired man. His skin was as white as marble and soft as a woman's. Don't, George, please. What would my husband say if he came in to find us like this after all these years? He trusts you, George. The nurses called him "Angelface" and "Little Cherub," because he was so soft and delicate looking. But I didn't ever, because he didn't smile, and his quiet way and stand-offishness gave me gooseflesh. He wasn't jolly, wasn't natural, the way I like folks. He was never rude, oh no, but just reserved, and not a spark of human nature in him, I thought. I suppose I was a noisy one: I've always believed in cheering them up. But when he came around, I couldn't. He made me feel awkward and silly because of his superior look. He never said anything against me, mind you. I could have taken him up, if he had. He was just a wet rag on everything I did. Well, one evening, which I had off—I remember it was a Wednesday, because it was early-closing day in those parts, which annoyed me—I was walking down the steps of the hospital when Levy came down beside me, dressed, as he used, in a close-fitting black coat with

ABOUT LEVY

a velvet collar. He had a thin body like a girl's. I said to him, just for a lark, mind, "Where are you going, doctor?" He said, "I'm going to the cinema to see *Intolerance*." "Oh, are you?" I said, "that's funny, because I'm going there too." Then, when he didn't say anything, I said, "May I come with you?" He said, "Yes, certainly, if you wish, Miss Smith." That was my name before I married, you know, but at the hospital they all called me "Janey." "All the others call me 'Janey,'" I said, "why don't you?" "I thought 'Miss Smith' suited you very well," he said, "but I will call you 'Janey' if it gives you any pleasure." "I don't believe you like me," I said. "What has led you to think that?" he said. "You think I'm too loud," I said, "and maybe you're right. But you've got to keep the people around you amused. Really I'm quiet by nature, but I make myself jolly for their sakes." "Why should you mind what I think of you?" he said. "I just like to be liked," I said. "Oh," he said, and we came to the cinema. He bought the tickets. "Oh," I protested, "I didn't mean that when I asked if I could come with you." "It's quite all right, Miss Smith," he said. "Call me 'Janey,'" I said. "What do they call you at home?" "I haven't got a home," he said; "my parents are dead." "I'm sorry," I said. That made me feel like a mother to him, though he was older than me. "You needn't be," he said, cross, and we went inside. It was ever so dark, and I caught hold his hand so's not to be lost from him. D'you know,

ABOUT LEVY

when he felt my hand in his he squeezed it so hard I nearly screamed. I never thought he had the strength in that little hand of his. No, George, you mustn't be impatient. I must wait for the butcher to come before we do anything, because I've got to give him a message about to-morrow's meat. I know it's unsatisfactory, but if you can't afford to get a room we can go to, like other couples, you must expect these little inconveniences. When we sat down, he said, "My name is Claude." "What a nice name," I said. He said, "I think it's a dreadful name." "There's no pleasing you," I said; "it's very uncommon. I've never met a boy called Claude before." "I've never met a girl named Smith before," he said. "Lord," I said, "you can't have met many girls, then." "I haven't," he said. Then the people in front said, "Sh," so I put my hand on his knee to comfort him, because I really was sorry for him. We were sitting right at the back, with just the curtains behind us; but, there were people standing, who pushed them on one side to see the film. He didn't seem to mind, but I wouldn't let him kiss me till they were gone. He'd got no sense of decency. Now, there's the butcher. You go upstairs to your room, George, and I won't be a moment now.'

George rose languidly, stubbed out his cigarette and went upstairs.

6. In her Orpen dress, velvet despite the heat, as she had been painted and hung on the line, Janet held the stocks in one hand and a vase in the other. She looked as slim as if she had never had a child; she was wearing her own hair, as there was an hour till lunch. She held them abunch, while she looked down at Miriam, who sat on a low chair, and then she walked to the small gate-leg. She had knocked—no, rather tapped lightly—on the door and opened before there could be an answer; a flouting little obeisance to privacy. So that no word had been spoken between them.

'I've come to do the flowers,' Janet said.

Then each continued her task without raising head or speaking. Janet stooped an instant over the flowers, cupping their scent between hands; her head and the short hair fallen, capped and held it to her face. Then she put the vase down, and stood looking at it, finger-tips to table, a leg bent and balanced on the toe.

She is being very theatrical with those flowers. It is

ABOUT LEVY

the first scene in a play. I'm not going to take any notice of her. That's also like the first scene in a play.

Janet did not turn as she said, 'So you didn't go, as you said.'

She stopped with a thread in the tapestry, a hand on the frame, and answered, 'No.' Then went on with her work.

Janet held the flowers in a ring of her first fingers and thumbs, shaking them into a casual bunch. She stood back with head cocking side and side, and said, 'I've got to say I never understood you and that little rat of a man; intrusive and subversive busybody, I thought him.'

Miriam was still working.

'It's just as well, I think, that he's got himself into this trouble. It will at least put an end to this stupid business.'

The mother looked at her daughter's back. She was sitting very straight in the low seat, like a child with a back-board. Now had stopped working.

'Once and for all,' she went on. 'Now you'll be be free to do as you like and choose as you like. There'll be no more nonsense about not marrying because of him.'

'When did I ever say that?'

'If you didn't say it, it was how you've acted all along.'

'I wouldn't marry him. I didn't want to.'

'Why not?'

'He didn't want marriage. He told me so.'

ABOUT LEVY

'Yet he proposed to Edith Mason. How can you account for that?'

Miriam did not answer immediately; then she said, 'I suppose he was doing something he didn't want.'

Janet walked over towards her. 'Don't talk nonsense. People never do anything they don't want to do. You know. They can't.'

'Yes, that's true in a way. But the reason why he proposed to Edith Mason was because he thought he must; not for selfish reasons, but because he had to get her away from Hall, and she had to have someone to look after her.'

Janet laughed. 'To look after her. *She* was looking for someone to look after. That's the cock-and-bull story he told in court. You don't believe that.'

'He told me too. I do believe it.'

'You can't believe it. You must see it's impossible.'

'I do believe it, and I believe, too, that it's better to take a person's word as to what he's done than to listen to someone else who scarcely knows him and is prejudiced against him.'

Janet went to the door. There was a large sentimental Christian poster on the wall by the door, of fat little children against a wash-blue sky, a thing Miriam bought from a friend while she was still at school. Eliphas, who pretended to be indifferent about religion, was annoyed at it.

'There's no need to take my words if you think me

ABOUT LEVY

prejudiced. Take the evidence of your own eyes. Edith Mason's beautiful. She's not clever; not got a fine soul, but she's beautiful, all right. If he asked her to marry him, there's only one reason why he did so.'

Miriam was going on with her work.

'And though he may be kidding himself, there's no reason for you to be taken in. What he says to you is one thing. He doesn't feel you as a woman. You don't let him. He tells you what he wants to be. But he shows her what he really is. You must remember *she* is beautiful.'

Miriam was going on with her work, but her shoulders were shaking. As the door closed she let the needle drop, walked over the the couch and lay down.

7.   RED, buoyant-bellied Mr. Mason floated from the side towards the centre of the bath. He held his head upright, looking up the slope of his body. His hands swirled the water without splashing. Moving slowly through the heavy salt, he came near to the lady with the red rubber cap. From this helmet small strands of hair escaped about her face. He liked her. She had rheumatism, too.

She turned round and smiled at him. He was expected and welcome.

They floated gently, side to side.

'I've read my paper this morning,' she said. 'I'm awfully sorry. What your child must be going through!'

'She must be suffering terribly,' Mason said, 'with only her mother there to help her. Of course, she needs a man's help, and here am I, fixed in Droitwich, unable to go to her.'

'I sympathise with you,' Mrs. Failey said. 'But you mustn't go. You've got your health to consider.

ABOUT LEVY

Besides, I don't know that I could bear you to leave me: I've come to depend on you.'

A rough fellow passed, splashing, who had come there for pleasure, not in pain. Mrs. Failey cried out. There was water in her eye. She was blinded.

'Unmannerly cub,' Mason said, and took her hand. Together they waded through the brine; Mrs. Failey whimpered. He got her under the shower and pulled the plug. The cold water sluiced over her face and down her shoulders. She smiled and cried and laughed with the shock of the cold water and joy.

Mr. Mason smiled and admired.

They parted to the ladies' and gentlemen's tiring-rooms and met again at the door, swaddled in towels, Electra's hot wraps.

He asked, 'Coffee in twenty minutes' time?'

Now she is gone to drink healing salt into her pores. She lies as I do, so prone on such a couch. Man can do limited amount of good; some find they do it best at home, others abroad. Besides, Edith is a selfish girl, and her mother has put her against me. Just because of the business in Trouville, which was never really satisfactory, with Mrs. Holt.

He did not have to wait long for Mrs. Failey in the refreshment-room. They sat in a corner away from where the wireless played.

'Would you like to tell me all about it?' Mrs. Failey said. 'It might make you feel easier in yourself.'

ABOUT LEVY

He stirred his coffee and looked grave. 'Well, I told you the other day how sad my home life has been, and how Winifred alienated my daughter from me when I had to go to Trouville to recover from my operation.'

'It made me feel so unhappy that I didn't sleep all night.'

'You see, then, I don't count for much with my family. I've only got to say a thing for them to decide to do the opposite. I knew both Christopher Hall and Claude Levy. Chris was a young good-for-nothing. He tried to get into the army and was turned down. Then he tried the law, and wasted his father's money for three years without passing one of his examinations. Then his father put him into business—leather, as far as I remember. He was on a month's trial. He was punctual for the first four days. Then he grew later every day. They didn't have to dismiss him at the end of the month, because he didn't turn up at all after three weeks. His parents couldn't find him; he'd left his lodgings.'

'How dreadful!'

'The colonel, his father, was very worried, because he used to drink too much, and during these fits he grew morbid and once tried to commit suicide.'

'Really?' said Mrs. Failey. 'Why didn't they bring that out in the trial?'

'It was hushed up. Nobody knew about it.'

'How did you find out, then?'

'Edith told me. He used to threaten to commit

ABOUT LEVY

suicide if she wouldn't marry him. Then she made him promise not to.'

'But they asked her if he had ever threatened to do so. Levy said he had, but she denied it.'

'Did she? I'd forgotten that. Well, I'm telling you about them. Where had I got to?'

'He disappeared.'

'Yes, he disappeared, and they couldn't find him. But he turned up again after three months, very shabby, asking for money.'

'What had he been doing all that time?'

'Working behind a bar in a public-house for his drinks and living on the wages of a shop-girl.'

'He was a bad lot.'

'Bad lot's what I always said; he was a wrong 'un. But they didn't listen to me. When I was a boy, if anyone behaved like that they were just shipped off to the colonies to live as remittance men. But not now. Now they take them back and give them not one chance but a dozen more chances, and then some. Well, he met Edith. If there's one thing can be said for her, it's that she's got looks. She may be selfish and sulky and proud—but she looks well.'

'She's a real beauty,' Mrs. Failey said, 'to judge from the paper, and I can see where she gets her looks from.'

'Well, her mother was a handsome woman when she was young—a handsome woman, you know. But she's old now, very old-looking. Well, this young Hall fell for Edith proper. She had him

ABOUT LEVY

there.' Mr. Mason held his hand out and tapped the palm. 'She held herself firm, didn't give way an inch to his pressure. She managed him and made him give up drink. A regular little reformer she became, and no mistake.'

'Not for long. But she sounds a good girl.'

'Oh yes, good, if you like to call good what's merely not being able to feel like common humanity does. She was a good girl, and he asked her to marry him. She didn't answer at first, and said it depended on how he behaved. The Halls, when they saw what power she'd got over him, wanted her to accept, and said that, if she would, they'd settle a house and fifteen hundred a year on him.'

'That was generous enough.'

'Generous! When I married I hadn't a third of that, and the little pile I've made I earned with the work of my hands and my honest brain's labour. But they're rich from an old stock, and fifteen hundred a year and a house was a cheap way to be respectably rid of a family nuisance. It was a good bargain. They were engaged.'

'You make it sound very mercenary.'

'Yes, you're right, though the money weighed with her. He was the sort of man she wanted, the hard type wants—somebody to marry and manage and condescend to, but never give themselves away to; the sort that will never give themselves utterly up to a man; as the Scriptures have it, they're afraid to lose their souls for fear of not finding 'em again.'

ABOUT LEVY

'Is this kind?' she said. 'Ought you to say it of your own daughter? Isn't it just theory?'

'Just theory, of course. But, as she's my own daughter, I ought to know, and I'm telling you. And about theory, the longer I live the more I believe it's theory that makes the difference between people; and that makes one person more worth than another. Clothes make the difference, they say, but theory's the mind's clothing. The same things are before your eyes and mine; but they see different things in them. How much we see depends on how much we can see; and that on how much we've seen before and really understood, which goes to make our theory. Everything we think and do is theory, I say, or based on it—right theory or wrong, but always theory.'

She sipped her coffee while he talked.

'That's just theory, also,' she said. 'You knew Claude Levy too?'

'Yes. Edith met him through me. At home I go to the bridge club most nights just for a little play; can't stand sitting at home. Rests me to meet people. A man I know there, Wilcox, introduced me to Claude at his home. That's where we met the first few times. He was quiet and didn't talk much usually. Then he'd suddenly break out and gabble. For instance, the first night after dinner Wilcox came out with a sneery remark about Socialism. I forget what it was, but something about nationalisation of banks. Wilcox is a bank manager, you know. This

ABOUT LEVY

little fellow pricked up and said, "The only reason why you object to it, Wilcox, is because you've got a good job and are afraid of losing it." That was what we all felt, but we didn't say it. "A very good reason too," Wilcox said. "If it's such a good reason," Levy answered, "why pretend that you disagree with nationalisation on high moral rather than personal grounds." It was funny the change that came over him when he talked; he was all energy. What he said was good sense too.'

'What else did he say?'

'Well, he said that everybody had been worrying too much about political liberty; getting a vote and having the rulers you vote for yourselves. They'd forgotten about personal liberty. I mean, that we resented any political or economic restrictions being placed on us, but accepted the most extraordinary social and moral restraints without a murmur. I remember he said that society was ruled by a tyranny of reactionary opinion. I liked that phrase.'

'So you asked him home?'

'Yes. That was four years ago. Edith was quite a child then, just turned eighteen. I never understood him with her. He came to talk to *me*, but she would come in and listen. I knew it wasn't to see me that she came. She seemed to depend a great deal on him and his opinion. But, you know, I never found out that she used to go and see him on Sunday afternoons till I read it in the papers. I shouldn't have allowed that with a girl of her age. I once asked her what she

ABOUT LEVY

thought of him; he was a Jew, you see, and I was afraid she'd want to marry him. "Well," she said rudely, "is it any concern of yours?" When I said it was, she said, "Because he's not a man, but just a person." '

'That was a queer thing to say.'

'What did it mean? It couldn't mean anything. It was just a clever thing to put me off—the sort of trick she learnt from her mother.'

Mrs. Failey looked at her watch again and said, 'Time for lunch.'

'What a time I've been talking,' he said. 'You lead me on.'

Then they got up, and Mason took her arm and led her across the road to the hotel.

8.   A DULL staircase thrust down towards the front of the room. Boots struck on the prismatic panes of street grating. Twined with noise of cups and shrill cooing of waitresses, clap and clop of shoes shelled in the place. The room was L-shaped, tiled tables jutted at right angles from the walls. A few men sat at table,—men without offices, talking business and drawing plans. They knew which was Betty and which Norma; were the regulars, and given three biscuits with their Bovril instead of two. A mother and two children, tired and tiresome, reproved one another. By the bar at the junction of the L, behind which a curved girl always wiped the counter after each cup of tea she made with spouting hot water, Mrs. Mason sat with her daughter. They each ate a macaroon.

'It's nearly over now,' Mrs. Mason said. 'I shall be glad when it's finished, for your sake and my own.'

The strain had softened her; after this she would be ill for weeks. It would give her indigestion.

ABOUT LEVY

Worry always did. But now she was too tired to be ill.

Edith was still bright, hard and firm, a gem. Looked as fresh and clear as she had been when she had given evidence. She had dreamed to be a witness with excitement. Gave her evidence impersonally, as though she had always been or was now incapable of feeling emotion. Her success was immediate with the jury; she captured them, as some actresses their audiences as soon as they come on the stage; there was no moment of hesitation or doubt of success.

'Do you think Claude will be condemned?' she said.

'I don't know. He ought to. He seems to me too wicked to live. The more I think of it, the more I realise how careful one has got to be. Of course, he was one of your father's friends.'

'At first I wasn't certain he'd done it. Do you know, I thought for an instant that Chris was capable of taking his own life. But when I remembered his promise—he swore to it on the Bible, you know, his gospel oath—and when I remembered his face as he swore it, of sudden freedom and joy, I knew that he couldn't have done it. You know that sketch that I drew of him, which you said was too flattering and romantic? That was how he looked when he swore that oath. It wasn't flattering at all. I drew what I saw in his face then. Now, if Chris did away with himself, the last year and that look of his, and my ideal of what he really was, would be false and wasted. I should have been taken in by him and swindled. It can't be possible.'

'How do you know it's impossible, dear?'

'By the surest proof. I feel that otherwise I couldn't live. I should be too ashamed to, for one thing, and for another my whole hope would be gone. But as Claude killed him out of jealousy, for that I am sure of, whether they convict him or not, Chris will always be what I thought him, the finest thing which I conceived in my imagination and which he was becoming; and became!'

Mrs. Mason broke off and munched the corner of her macaroon. She did not follow Edith's words, in pity at loss for a more definite emotion.

Then Edith said suddenly, 'Why has it all happened? Why isn't Chris still alive and Claude my friend? He was the only person I could rely on.' *This excludes me, her mother.* 'My world's turned upside down, but the whole world moves and will go on unchanged. What I held dearest has no longer any value for me, but is the interest of every paper. God, nothing will survive or matter after this.'

'Remember where you are, dear,' Mrs. Mason said.

She saw the men at one table stop talking and look in their direction. They looked and turned and nodded. Edith couldn't see them. Her head was bent over the table. She was crying.

One of the men, dapper—he had brown and white

suède shoes—came over to them and bowed and said, 'May I get you a taxi, Mrs. Mason?'

'Yes, please,' she said. *How did he know my name?*

Betty and Norma came around.

'Go away,' Edith said. 'Tell them to go away.'

Mrs. Mason got her check and said, 'Thank you, my daughter will be better in a little while.'

The taxi was at the door. The dapper man stood waiting. As they got in, Betty and Norma ran up the stairs to see them again. The men had said who they were.

The polite man who had fetched the taxi went into a telephone-box and twirled the dial. Then he said, 'Hallo, is that Pollock? *Re* Levy case, take this down: "I suggest the headline 'Plucky Edith's Collapse after Eleven-day Ordeal . . .' but that's your business. . . .' "

9. 'MEMBERS of the jury, you have a difficult and weighty case to try. In coming to your decision, you must remember and constantly hold in mind the gravity of the issues involved. It has been, and is the proudest boast of a citizen of this country, that when an allegation is made against his conduct, and a charge is brought, he must be regarded as innocent until the contrary be proved. It is possible that certain of you have read matter printed in the daily press purporting to give the facts of this case. If that is so, I beg and implore you to expel from your minds anything that you may have read or heard or yourselves spoken with regard to this case, either before or during the proceeding of this trial, and I urge you, recollecting only what has been allowed in evidence, to bring the uttermost impartiality of mind to weigh the arguments of counsel based upon that evidence. Furthermore, I would have you remember that if the scales of justice are weighted at all, they are weighted in favour of the accused and not against him; that is to say, that while a particle of reasonable

ABOUT LEVY

doubt remains in your mind, you must not return the verdict of guilt.

'The case before you is remarkable because it contains almost no dispute of fact except of the one essential fact, and yet the interpretation of each fact is disputed.

'The facts of the case simply and clearly are as follows: At about five o'clock on the afternoon of May the eighteenth, the accused, Dr. Claude Levy, called on the deceased, Christopher Hall, at his flat. There was no one in the flat except these two men. At six o'clock, Mrs. Trandle, the housekeeper, entered the flat with her own key and found her master lying dead on the floor of the sitting-room with the accused kneeling beside him. This is the only evidence that we have apart from that of the accused himself; and expert witnesses.

'The accused gives the following account of the hour which he spent in the deceased's flat. Although he was the deceased's doctor, he had not come to see him in his professional capacity. On entering, he placed his hat and practitioner's bag on a table in the hall. This table was placed next to the door of the sitting-room, and the bag was on that end of the table nearest the door. They then both went into the sitting-room, and as they went the accused maintains that some such conversation as this occurred. The deceased, "Strange to see you at this time." The accused, "Came in on my way to poison a dog." He asserts that this was a joking half-statement; he was to call on a patient who lived in the next street, and incidentally to poison her dog for her. You have heard Mrs. Holme state in evidence that she had asked the accused if he would poison her dog for her, and that he had promised he would.

'The accused saw that Hall had been drinking; it was obvious both from his manner and a half-finished bottle of whisky that stood on the table. Knowing that Hall suffered from valvular disease of the heart he warned him that he should not drink any alcohol at all, and that, taken in such quantities as he did take it, it might well prove fatal. He says that he had spoken to him on numerous occasions, but without effect. The post-mortem revealed that the accused's diagnosis was correct.

'Before he proceeded to the business which he had come to discuss, he went to the sideboard, on which he saw standing the tear-glass which you have seen. To collect glass, especially drinking glasses, was a hobby of the accused's which he had in common with the deceased. He picked this glass up,—he cannot say whether by the stem or just beneath bowl,—and held it up to the light and tapped it; while he did so, he talked with the deceased about where he had bought it; shops they knew which sold old glass; and bargains they had recently driven. Then they sat down, and Hall offered the accused a drink, which he refused.

'In order to understand the relation of the accused to the deceased, you must remember, members of the jury, that some time previously the deceased, again under the influence of alcohol, had told him, from some obscure impulse of braggadocio, that he had committed murder. Asked how Hall had come to make such a confession to him, the accused said that he had had considerable personal power over Hall, which as his doctor he had used to strengthen the weakness of character which was responsible for the conduct that was undermining his health. When he learnt that he was going to marry Miss Mason, a young woman for whom he, the accused, had the greatest respect, he tried even harder to "patch Hall up into something which resembled a man." On the occasion referred to, having tried all sympathetic methods of restoring Hall's self-respect without success, he tried abuse to see if he could arouse it in that way. In the course of this treatment the accused said Hall was a drunkard and a weakling, incapable even of committing a crime. It was then that the accused got the opposition he desired. Hall asserted that this was not true: he had committed murder. The accused did not believe him, because he was drunk. But when Hall came round the next morning at six o'clock and begged him not to disclose what he had said the night before, he thought there was more in it. He gave a promise of secrecy, but did not scruple to use the hold that the possession of this knowledge gave him over Hall's conduct.

'At this interview on May the eighteenth the two men sat talking for some time, about three-quarters

ABOUT LEVY

of an hour. The accused says that he urged Hall not to marry Miss Mason. The deceased answered that his only chance lay in marrying her. The accused said that if he did so he would certainly sacrifice her to his weakness. If he intended to change his way of life, he must change it before marriage, and as an earnest he must tell her that he had committed murder. With such a secret undisclosed the marriage could not be anything but a failure. Hall said that it would not make any difference. The accused answered that, if that were so, he could have no objection to telling her.

'Hall would not face the issue; he was a coward. The accused admitted under cross examination that he tried to bully Hall either to confess or not to marry; and that he thought the event in either case would be the same, that, as he wished, the marriage would not take place. Hall, who was drinking all the time, said, "No one will know that I killed anyone or, at any rate, till I'm dead." The accused says that he kept trying "to fix Hall's attention with his eyes" and "impose his will on him," but that he could not do so, because Hall's energies were "dispersed by alcohol."

'The accused maintains that at about this time he had a fit of coughing, and the deceased got up and left the room with the tear-glass, saying that he would fetch him some water. He walked with the slight sway of a man under the influence of alcohol. The prisoner ceased coughing before the deceased returned, and called out that there was no longer any need for the water. Hall shouted back that he would come in in a moment. The accused sat for a time reading the newspaper of the previous evening, and heard Hall cross the passage from the kitchen to the lavatory, pull the plug and return immediately to the kitchen, where he remained a moment. He did not know what Hall did in the kitchen, because of the noise of the cistern refilling; but after a very short time Hall came back into the sitting-room. He was staggering, but succeeded in reaching his chair before collapsing. All that he said after that was, "When I am dead, they may all know." This he repeated almost inaudibly. The accused says that he now realised that something was gravely wrong. He thought at first that it was merely excess of alcohol; but finding that consciousness did not lapse, but the pain merely increased, he saw that it was something more serious. He asked Hall what was the matter, but received no answer. He was clutching his hand into his stomach, and seemed to be in too much pain to speak. Thinking that it was perhaps a heart attack brought on by the alcohol, the doctor tried artificial respiration. He again asked him what was wrong and where the pain was, but the deceased could not or would not speak.

'He went out for his bag and, finding it missing, went into the kitchen, where he saw it on the table, open, and the glass standing on the slip-board of the sink. There was a small quantity of water and a slight deposit in the bottom of the glass. A sniff at it confirmed the suspicion that his open bag had aroused.

'He returned to the sitting-room, where he found the deceased unconscious. He died soon after, without recovering consciousness. Before the accused could notify anyone, Mrs. Trandle entered. As soon as he saw her, the accused said to her, "Mr. Hall has taken poison; I am going for the police." Mrs. Trandle said in evidence that the accused appeared excited, his hands were shaking and his face was white. Mrs. Trandle added that she heard him say, "It was my fault. I ought not to have done it. *I poisoned him myself.*" On being cross-examined by counsel for the defence, she admitted that she was not very certain of the last sentence, "I poisoned him myself." The accused admits to having said, "It was my fault. I ought not to have done it." He meant that it was his fault to have brought a bag containing poisons to Hall's flat, and that he ought not to have bullied Hall in the way that he had. The sentence that Mrs. Trandle had misheard and misreported was, "I might as well have poisoned him myself," which need not imply that he wished to murder Hall, but merely that he felt that by having the poison in his bag and accentuating Hall's suicidal state of mind, he was tantamount to Hall's murderer, though, in fact, he was not his murderer. Mrs. Trandle said she did not think those were the words used, because she had a clear impression that he had

ABOUT LEVY

confessed to having poisoned Hall. When she was asked why in that case she had let the accused leave the flat to call the police, the witness said that he was gone before she could collect her senses.

You may think the value of Mrs. Trandle's evidence is inconsiderable, that perhaps, without realising it, she is inclined to exaggerate out of a love of the sensational, to please the prosecution, by whom she has been called, or from inability to discriminate between truth and falsehood. But you must remember that it is possible that, though her recollection of the words spoken by the accused is indefinite, her impression of their implication may be correct. And, furthermore, even though the accused may not have admitted guilt at the time, this does not prove that he is innocent.'

10. 'Well, if it isn't my Diddlums,' Hill said. 'Back from Africa?'

'Yes,' Common said, 'back from Africa. But I'm surprised to see you here.'

'I always come to Commemoration Day. I haven't missed once since I was chaplain.'

'Yes, I remember that. But I thought you'd have been in London with Claude.'

'Oh, I see. Do you know, I haven't seen Claude for years; he broke completely away from me.'

'Is that so?'

There was a silence.

'How does England appear to a visitor from abroad?' Hill said.

'It all seems to be much too small; especially this place. I suppose so much of the time was spent actually in the grounds that it made them seem vast; we did so much that seemed important at the time. We'd think nothing of it now.'

'Yes.'

'But everything seems very small in comparison with Africa; the scale of the landscape and the plants—everything.'

ABOUT LEVY

'What did you think of Bobby Rudlands' sermon? Of course, he was before your time.'

'A long while before. I don't really know about sermons; I hear so few. But the ones I do hear I can't understand. I'm no good at mathematics either.'

'What do you mean?'

'Well, there are two sorts of sermons: there's the kind directed against prevalent abuses and giving practical guidance. I can't understand those, because I never know what the abuses are which the preacher refers to, and his practical guidance seems to be the blind leading the purblind. The other sort is exegetic, and, honestly, I prefer anagrams.'

'I should have thought "sacrifice" and "service," the keynotes of the Bishop's address, were simple and fine enough ideas for anyone.'

'I thought I understood them in the days when I thought these playing-fields were big. But this idea of sacrifice seems to me more and more difficult to understand.'

Hill didn't want to be drawn in, but couldn't help it. He said, 'Nonsense. There's no difficulty, that I can see.'

Common was looking at him, and his mouth was firm and serious, but his eyes were laughing at him. 'It's not my idea,' he said, 'nor a new one.' 'Claude put it into my head when I was here. It was probably not original in him. I've found that a lot of the things he said to me weren't original; but what he said in this case was, that to be Christian was not to be

ABOUT LEVY

Christlike (as I think St. Paul tells us to be), but to be Christ. Christ himself was not a Christian in the sense that you try to be, because he didn't conform himself to a model, but was his own prototype. For him death on the cross wasn't an act of love or of sacrifice, but the supreme act of devotion to a purpose, for the achievement of which he was prepared even to die. When people saw that from outside, they called it an act of self-sacrifice, though for him it was not self-sacrifice, but self-fulfilment. You know that a child, when it's set its heart on something, counts all the things that it usually values worthless until it has achieved or obtained what it has set its heart on. I understand what I call Christ's suicide as a neglect of all other things for the achievement of a single purpose; not an abnegation of desires, but a concentration of them on a single object.'

'We're getting very deep,' Hill said, 'and rather unorthodox. It's perhaps as well you decided not to enter the priesthood.'

'I think I'm too serious-minded,' Common said.

'Are you coming to the Speeches?'

'No, they're always dull; lot of old fools patting one another on the back. I want to take a look round this place again. It's changed very little.'

'Couldn't afford to change. Well, so long, Diddlums. That's what I used to call you, you remember.'

Hill walked off with hands in pockets. There

ABOUT LEVY

were so many people to see on Commemoration Day. To each, he talked of the last. But behind his talk there remained in his consciousness the figure of Claude at different moments of his guardianship; when his mother died; when he first came to the vicarage. He kept to his room as much as he could when he was in the house. Not making a nuisance of himself as boys should, but quietly reading or drawing figures in armour. He knew the uniform of every soldier and collected regimental badges. But he didn't draw modern soldiers, but mediaeval knights and Roman soldiers and gladiators.

He used to hide when I came in. Remember I opened the door of the study, a heavy door, and swung it back to feel something soft. It didn't hit the stop, but crushed his body against the wall. He was hiding then; wasn't I amazed to see him crouching there when I pulled the door back? I didn't let him in because of that Decameron, and I didn't want him routing among my things anyway. I said, 'What do you mean by coming in here?' He didn't speak. I caught hold of his ear and pulled his head down; he was a little worm. It did me good to feel my hand fit on his skull when I hit him. Then he wriggled out and ran under my arm and upstairs to his room. It makes me laugh to think how silly he looked. And the door was locked when I went up. It wasn't again, though. Remember I found the key the other day useless among a box of others. Then again the same thing happened, didn't it? it was quite a little habit when Mother Willis came, who liked him.

ABOUT LEVY

I saw the french window from my chair and a dirty hand go up to the handle and turn it. He didn't make a sound, I must say, but the door opened very slowly and shut again. And I couldn't see him. Saw nothing till a hand and boot under the table. I let him get nearly to the door before I called him. 'Claude, what are you doing? Here's Mrs. Willis, who wants to see you. Don't you want to speak to her?' I didn't look round, just called. The old lady was a bit surprised, I could see. She stopped talking, and there was no noise. Then I looked up to the ceiling, as if he was in the room above, and called again, 'Claude, Claude,' and she looked up to the ceiling fairly amazed. And I said, 'Why don't you stand up like a man instead of skulking there like a little dog?' Funny, I seemed to blush, the blood was in my face. He got up then when I said 'skulking like a little dog,' walked over and shook hands with her and tried to turn and go from the room. But I couldn't let him go like that. When he was at the door, and had his hand on the handle, I said, 'Claude, you haven't apologised to Mrs. Willis for your extraordinary behaviour.' He did that, and then I let him go. Yes, I think that cured him.

While he listened to the speeches and to Bubb whispering ecclesiastical gossip, and while the band played Mendelssohn, the same selection as they had twenty years ago because Sir George liked it—new fiddlers and a new pianist, but the same fiddle, the old grand, the old, old 'cello—he thought of Claude at school. Hill always sat in the same place, on the middle gangway in the second row. He had sat

ABOUT LEVY

there to watch Claude each year take prizes. He used to take as many as he liked. Now different boys went for prizes and bowed; and one as usual, like Claude, went up to the platform so many times that there were special plaudits and laughs, and a little of the admiration which is given to the best athlete. He thought of Claude's mental ability with the exaggerated wonder of one who has none. When he compared this image with that of Claude in the box, he wondered whether he ought not to be in court with him. Then he thought that if Claude were condemned, as he certainly would be, he would visit him in prison and offer him the consolation of religion. The plan burned in mind and warmed him. It was an illumination, a divine message. He wanted to walk out of the room and shout with joy.

The speaker would not stop. He was a cleric and a don; he went on making clerical donnish jokes at which the parents laughed, most of them were parsons and wished they were dons.

Hill grew cold. He remembered the Mothers' Union Meeting, the Boys' Club, the Women's Guild, the early visitation of his Bishop. It was not a divine message, but a silly idea. He really couldn't go then. Now if only it had been last week. Anyway, his guardianship had ended when Claude was twenty-one.

11. *His face hasn't changed; is the same chapped red. I got off the boat, when? Two days ago. Claude I saw last at the station, going back to Africa, I waving from the carriage with a paper and he waving beneath a lamp which swung and lit and shaded his face alternate instants. Now he's in dock, poor blighter. He'd keep calm; they'd never tell what he was feeling. Mackenzie said it was just exhaustion that made the man seem callous in the box; and the shifting points of focus. Coming here's like a long walk to see a house you knew; remember the mill-house; and the lane's the same, and grocer and parson the same; but they didn't know me. And what I'd come to see was gone. They'd driven a new road over it. Some of the bricks were in the bridge. More like in dreams, when there isn't such a place. This seat's the same, damn it. What's he done? He said, 'You're me in Africa; we're on the same stunt, but the place makes the difference. Control must be physical in primitive communities. I use mind where you use body and revolver.' I use mind. To kill? Not to kill, but to*

ABOUT LEVY

control. Killing is my form of control. Of course, 's got to be. Remember Black Jackson; was what a low-breed means. Wasn't his fault though; it was the missionaries got him to the coast; whisky did the rest. Got used to white men's houses. Was in prison for theft. That did him in as it did in the big chap McDougal told me about. Warder said he went sort of dead, while he was there. Always shagging himself. Twisted his spirit, but didn't break it. Not a long enough sentence. 'I couldn't bear 'is look,' warder said; 'he was so quiet, got on my nerves, eyes turned up as if he was trying to look into th' back of his head.' Can see 'im. But he was different when I met him, when he went back to 'is people. Energy leapt in him, but it was turned against us. Bound to cause trouble. And he wandered around, trying to get back with them. They let him be. Too quick and talked too much for 'em. Remember that fellow on the boat who talked too much, and I felt sick seeing this about Claude on the news-sheet; one of them damn planters, talking about his bloody crops and when they'd be 's mature 's Virginian. Then he got back though and was chief and had 'em under 'is thumb. I knew it by the faces; he got 'em turned up round on me. Not even the boys let on. Know those gaps you come to with 'em. You're free with 'em and easy, and they talk as if you're one of them. Then a gap, don't know what sort, of time or continuity. You're strangers ultimately. In the village they moved with that angular movement of hostility—limbs sort of furred with resentment. This valley here's so quiet with the sheep

ABOUT LEVY

grazing and the caw of rooks. Jerky when I went down to speak to him. I'm sure ammunition is being smuggled in to the village. No, oh no, his smiling mouth. Saw his head nod 'No' before I asked. No, bowing and cringing, when he could have had me taken and shot then. His energy'd been forced underground. Could 've said 'Yes,' and had me taken. But was a coward in the open; agoraphobia. Hours in prison twisted the spirit under earth. Then I had him; held him in my hand as this match, to snap as I wished. Snap and throw down and be done with. We both saw that before I turned, when I told him that though it hadn't happened it must stop. Yet I didn't know then if he'd shoot me as I left. Remember thinking to be shot in the back and fall and they cluster about: remember saying, 'It's not me he fears, but all white men.' I took his hand and squeezed it, shaking it, shook his whole body down towards me with my arm's power: and weakness flickered his eyes around. Remember thinking if I turn round he'll shoot; but think I'm sure of myself, if I don't; remember nodding, and raising hand to the men and wanting to look back and not looking back. God, it was good, when I heard for sure that the arms were coming in and there was joining of clans at that feast against us. Saw how the spines arched almost like cats. And I knew I'd got to clear him out. Before it was like being in training for fight, and never knew if it was coming off. And the boy went off to tell 'em from me I was coming down, and thought I was mad. The cleared street and no children about. Except behind the huts, peeping. Never heard such

ABOUT LEVY

silence. Yet I knew they all knew, and when I got to the hut they were all around me in a sort of club-shape, with me at the head; the great fine man at my side, that had been chief before him. I don't remember all these rooks; never noticed them when I was here. He wouldn't come out, and I cried 'Come out' in their lingo for 'em to know. They all looked at the door, waiting for him to come out. I thought he wouldn't; thought he was skulking, and cried out again, 'We are waiting. Are you afraid?' They were ashamed of him, and began to whisper and waver. I'd 've won them in a moment more. Then, remember his face, the paint and spear and shield. Was as old as his race, with them behind him. Didn't recognise him. Thought he would cringe out, but he was all strength of a sudden, body against my body. Could have had me then; I didn't know what or how. That 'oohing' and 'aahing' began. They were all his side, an' 'd 've killed me if he'd shown a sign. God, he was really new man then. But I thought the race-tide had reached a height and would ebb on him, leaving him stranded; anyway, I couldn't do anything. But that low crying of theirs pricked his soul up. Saw light catch in his eye like bush-fire. An' it was so quick and easy, the shot. Seemed to stand long, though, clutching the spout-blood till it crept through his fingers; then he fell. Can see now how he fell, heavy on his arm, and his leg kick in the dust, and that moment when he died. Eyes a snake's till the light hardened in them. It was a different silence from these fields. Suppose I knew they were all thinking more in

ABOUT LEVY

that moment than they were used to in a year. He was the centre, not me. We all looked at him, I a spectator; sort of oracle, twisted in the last throe. Odd, the paint wasn't part of him any longer, as if he and it had shrunk apart. False like make-up. Then they looked at me, and the old chief said, 'The white lord has done right.' Was that murder? ... How they took up the cry running their ranks along and merging and separating. It would be murder in the silence of these fields. 'The white lord has done right.' I look down at the sweat-black backs; I see them raise and carry and throw it out of the village; see the dogs following. But this rich grass under these oaks has another logic. He said, you can get cigarettes from the masters' common-room; and then I really will look round the place.

12. Ruth Abrahams took up the chinese bowl. She knew nothing of it; its value was vaguely great. It was the more precious because prized in the world: more valuable because he had given it to her. He brought it back on the second anniversary of their wedding. In the morning he had not mentioned their wedding-day or seen that there were roses on the table. She had spent all day miserable until he came home with the bowl. When she unwrapped it, she held it up for a moment only; then, putting it down, kissed him. She would not have cared how ugly it was, so long as there was a sign of remembrance. Nothing else mattered at the time.

She had carried it away to her room and put it on the table by the window; where it stood in the full light. After a few days she looked at it and saw what it was in itself, its form and blue shapes, its bluey whiteness. She saw this thing without his aid, and the curve's poise from base to lip. No longer only a memento, it had become an isolated thing, apart from

ABOUT LEVY

her husband and herself. It was not alive, but beyond living; seemed to have moved sinuously before it hardened.

She kept it in her room. David told her to put flowers in it so that it might be useful. But she withstood him in this; wanted it to remain free in her room.

When his will lay over hers, backed by his age and money and mind, she turned away from him and locked herself in her room. There she was alone with this other beauty, which demanded nothing and remained the same whether she looked at it or not. He had found her young, waited till she was old enough to marry; never held her in, but always encircled her. When she wanted to break away in any direction, he was always before her, saying, 'Yes, you can go there. You will find this or that there.' She went and found it. She was bound by a neck-noose; when she wanted to break it, he paid out the rope so that she could never get it taut.

She did not escape him in either of her sons. He could stand aside and wait his time. She had always to call him back. He came when he wanted. But she had no resistance. Men would willingly have helped to alter their tensions, so that he grasped and she bent back. But she was afraid, and could not trust the unseen logic of the spirit. She was afraid to lean back and let him come to her. She feared that in a nick he would be gone. So she did not play other men against him.

ABOUT LEVY

Even in the heaviness of the pregnancies, when her life turned inwards to the child, she was afraid he would go from her, and she came to the call like a heavy bitch to her master. And his will dominated the children. She was near to them, and they loved her better. But him they revered and obeyed without question. He was their sun and god. They lived on his gifts by his light.

So that the bowl was the only escape into impersonal peace; the locked door the only barrier against the intrusion of his will.

She held this bowl to her and learnt it with her hands. Thus to hold took her beyond husband and child, and would take her perhaps beyond what now pressed on her brain, thought of her brother.

But she could not forget him. What she thought she ought to feel clashed with her feelings. She should be upset, convinced that he was innocent; or if she could not be convinced, grieved that he should so have fallen into sin. Yet, holding this bowl, she knew that she was neither upset nor grieved, and didn't care whether he was guilty or not. Stronger than all else, joy obtruded, hope came forward; that he was guilty and would be condemned. Then he would be gone from her life, his overseeing struck blinded down. He would no longer be an eye round the corner nor scout from a high place. The seed of her life could swell and luxuriate unseen into new fruitfulness.

ABOUT LEVY

She put down the bowl on to its black carved stand. The wood stand, taking, held a lost forgetfulness. The old way was blocked to escape: a tree fallen across the rails, a sudden avalanche in a trusted cutting.

The noises of her day were about her: the plaintive whistle of tradesmen, the lift rattling, John beginning to cry and the nurse's coaxing scolding. But the door was shut between them and her. She was rapt into a sincerity, brought to a stop in flight. The foot checked too late, the hands up to fend, right into the buttoned breast of truth.

When Claude was twelve and she was eight, there had been war but no actual fighting. There was no physical touching, but a warfare in absence. She laid tin tacks on the path where he took his bicycle. She didn't know why: a blind fury to worst him, prevented her knowing. She did not know, but she still remembered the whole scene, its failure and her being shown up. It was taken before her mother, the ultimate court; she couldn't explain—it was incomprehensibly foolish. Earlier, before her father died, Claude with his small pocket-money bought her mother flowers every Saturday. With his pocket-money! Once she saw him take money from her mother's drawer. He came back then with a small bunch of roses. She knew he stole, but couldn't tell. It was against all rules, and she couldn't disclose it any other way. She said, 'They must have cost a lot,' and he answered,

ABOUT LEVY

'They did.' Shameless. But her mother took no notice except to kiss him. Perhaps she knew that he stole to buy her presents. Perhaps she didn't mind.

In retaliation he broke her dolls, of which she had a number. But it was not massacre. He broke only her favourites; cleverly, so that he was not found out. Or if he didn't break them, he hid them away so that she never knew whether the doll was destroyed or merely hidden. When she went to her mother and accused him, he asked her where she had left them. Often she couldn't remember. But when she said a place, the doll was there or near there. And her mother blamed her for carelessness. Once she left a doll on her bed, and when she complained to her mother in Claude's hearing, said she had left it in her doll's pram. Claude told her to go and look there. It was in the doll's pram. When she explained the trick to her mother, she was blamed both for forgetfulness and being suspicious. There was no justice.

Yet when Father died she won Mother over completely. She cried and captured her love. Her mouth then was wet with delight and body tingled with goodness. She was the girl in story-books, and because she was so kind and loving she held her mother's love.

But there was no complete triumph in this victory. Claude had turned away. It was a race between two horses in which one had scratched: a walkover. Claude had turned away from Mother. He did not like her weeping over his father, while she was sorry for her father's death and her feelings ran abreast of her mother's. She had loved him, and felt good to feel sorry. But Claude burnt the black clothes.

One morning they found the black dress burnt. She stood by without speaking, though since her father's death she had been able to speak with less check. It wasn't her age that had mattered, but the greater age of the people round her. She stood silent, appalled, and watched her mother and Claude face to face.

The violation to property shocked her, the wanton burning. Mother stood shaking, white, unable to deal with Claude. She said, 'Only say that you're sorry, and I'll forgive you.' He answered, 'I hate them. Why do you wear these ugly things? I won't say I'm sorry, because I'm not sorry. I'm glad.'

Ruth remembered she put in, tempting, 'What are you glad of?'

He shouted, 'I'm glad I've burnt them and I'm glad he's dead, too.'

Mother stood clenched still, as if controlling herself after being hit. Then quickly took him by the neck in rage, saying, 'You wicked, impious boy to speak so of your father'; bent down his neck so that his body right-angled at the hips. She seemed to get a new strength, but trembled so, that she could not undo his trousers. He, quivering also, let them down, exposing the white buttocks, braced

ABOUT LEVY

firm. She caught a shoe up and beat him, the flesh reddening under the strokes. They cannot have hurt much; they were too hurried. Mother beat in frenzy. But his face was set red, except a white mark where his teeth bit his lip.

Then suddenly the blows stopped. She dropped the shoe. Her hands, arms, whole body were shaking. In a sort of fit that terrified Ruth, she fell into a chair in a heap from which came cries of weeping, wrung sounds of caught breath.

Claude, who had not spoken, stood up and pulled up his trousers. The blood left his face. He tried to brace his buttons calmly. Ruth went to Mother and touched her shoulder, but there was no response. She came to Claude and said, 'You wicked boy! I wish you were dead.' Claude hit her with the open hand on the side of the head. The noise was greater than the hurt, but she fell. She meant to fall, and lay still so that he should think her dead. But he didn't wait to look at her. He went straight out, past Susan, who was bustling in. When he was gone Ruth began to cry. Susan took her up in arms and she yelled. When she was set down, almost melted with self-pity, she ran to her mother, crying 'Poor Mother, what can Susan do?' climbed onto her, and was received into her bosom, her forehead splashed with tears.

13.   Mrs. Bailey knocked at the door.

It stood open to air the house. Yet the draught that came through was laden with stench, rank of poverty. The children were playing in the passage and on the doorstep. She had to step between them to reach the hinged ring that served as knocker.

Straggle-haired, wiping red, dirt-lined hands on an old apron, Mrs. Handley came to the passage end.

'You, Mrs. Bailey? I wondered who it might be. The tally-man comes every day now for what's owin'. Bert's out waiting for his relief. But they swallow it up before the week begins, the dirty bastards.'

'Are you too busy to spare a minute?' Mrs. Bailey said. 'After what we said this morning, I went up and looked in the old chest. I've got things in there which would surprise you. My grandmother's veil—that was married to a sailmaker at Plymouth—which me mother wore when she was wed and me after her. It's laid in soft paper with moth balls, and fine as new, except it's better than you could buy now, such careful working.'

ABOUT LEVY

'Come in, Mrs. Bailey. And you, Reggie, stop grubbing in that there gutter. How many times have I told you? Come 'ere at once, come 'ere.'

Reggie crawled to his mother. A constant grey mucus oozed from one nostril. She wiped it with an old rag.

'There, keep on the pavement now,' she said. 'Come in, Mrs. Bailey, into the parlour. Children everywhere. What chance have the poor little nippers got in a house like this? I can't have 'em in the back when I'm washing. Where 've they got to play but in the gutter 'n the dirt?'

Mrs. Bailey went in. Mrs. Handley went away and came back in a moment without an apron, tidier, tucking in her hair with her hands.

'I brought these things,' Mrs. Bailey said. 'I had 'em in my chest.'

There was a bundle tied round with ribbon, of old letters, photographs, and post-cards.

'This was his hair, the first time it was cut, dark and curly as it is now, and very soft. His mother kept it; and when she died Father Hill, who didn't hold with such nonsense as he called it, was going to burn it till I asked him to give it me. When I saw young Claude last I showed it to him—that was the last time I looked at it myself till now—fifteen years ago it must be, when he was studying to be a doctor. He sat stooping over it as you do now, and I told him I was keeping it for the time he was married, to give it to his bride. He said, "I don't want to

ABOUT LEVY

marry." "There's many 've said that before," I said, "and changed their minds." And he changed his mind, like the rest, from what I've seen in the papers. But perhaps he won't marry now, at any rate not that girl, after the way he's treated her.'

'Or the way she's treated him. Bert says to me, "If ever girl wanted a man hanged, it's Edith Mason," 'e says; and 'e's right.'

'He's right. Not wild horses would move her, the hard face.'

'"For the sake of pride," I told 'im, "that girl would 'ave 'er own father hanged, if need be." When I was at the Feathers, there was a girl, Queenie, behind the counter with me, just such a one. She'd lie herself black to save her face; you couldn't tell whether she was lying or not except, as Mrs. Hole used to say, when Queenie lied it sounded more like the truth than when she didn't.'

'These are letters he wrote me when he was at college; see the pictures he drew of his masters. Comical, aren't they? So clever with his pen. Oh dear, they make me laugh now to see them. There's me with the great cake I made him for his birthday; it's that light, see, it's got wings like the advertisement for self-raising flour. These are post-cards that he wrote me, when he was on his holidays. See here, a foreign one, Belgique, Bruxelles—that's from Brussels, in Belgium. He went there just before he left off schooling. These are letters which he wrote me

ABOUT LEVY

every Christmas, when he sent me the turkey every year.'

'And you haven't seen him for fifteen years?'

'Fifteen years next Christmas it is, exact.'

'That's a long time.'

'It's a long time, Mrs. Handley but I expect it's shorter to me than it is to you.'

'Perhaps it is.'

'He asked if he could come and spend Christmas with me once. That letter must be here.'

She searched in the pile: but her eyes were weak and fingers fumbled. Mrs. Handley took them and found it.

'Let me read it,' Mrs. Bailey said. She held trembling glasses on her nose. ' "Dear Susan"—that's the name he called me by—"May I spend Christmas with you? I always regard your cottage as my real home. Last Christmas I went to see Ruth, who lives with my uncle and aunt. But they are Jews, and don't celebrate Christmas, so it was very dull. I am sending a turkey by the railway, so when it comes you will know who it's from. I will come down by the 3.25 on Christmas Eve, if that suits you. It arrives at Sudbury at 6.37. Now the war is over, we can let ourselves go. Will there be any of your lardy cakes? Father Hill wanted me to go and spend Christmas with him at Stoke, where he is now. But I wouldn't. Below is Father Hill carving Christmas dinner." Look, there he is cutting a great Christmas pudding and angels sitting

ABOUT LEVY

all round, and the devil with a tail sneaking a bit off one of the plates. Wasn't he a one?'

'He must have been indeed: and did he come?'

'He came just as he said, and we sat and laughed and talked of old times. But it wasn't very good somehow. He seemed restless, and 'ld be silent in the middle of our talking. I s'pose I was too old for him and not educated enough. When he went I said, "Have you enjoyed yourself, Master Claude?" And he said, "Call me just Claude, Susan," and kissed me and said, "Of course." I said, "You'll come again next year?" He said, "Of course" again. But he never came; he sends the turkey, but he'll never come.'

There was a knock.

'See who it is,' said Mrs. Handley; 'there's a dear.'

Mrs. Bailey gathered up the papers and went out into the passage. It was the baker.

'What is it?' she said.

The baker said, 'Two bob owing.'

She gave him a florin and went back into the room.

'Who was there?' Mrs. Handley said.

'No one,' Mrs. Bailey said. 'But I must go now. I'm keeping you from your work.'

14. Janey lay waiting, but George turned, looking at the ceiling. Flies were playing about the lamp-shade. Two intersecting cracks cut the ceiling in rough quarters. Some plaster hung imminent over the bed. Next time Mr. Jarvis moved his furniture round it would fall. George thought, if it fell now it would land on my belly; it would break on her hand, leaving a white mark. He leant over to his clothes and got a packet of Woodbines. He offered her one.

Though she said, 'I oughtn't to smoke yours,' she took one. He bent over her and lit it. She was annoyed, but he went on smoking. He was a man again, ready to look for work. He would get up in a short time and go to the Labour Exchange. The other men there were not so lucky. They were married and had children to keep.

As she lay waiting, she said, twining his hand with hers, 'George, what are you thinking?' Then again, 'Come, a penny for them.'

'Go on with what you said about Levy,' he said. 'I never knew before that you knew him.'

ABOUT LEVY

'How should I tell you with my husband by, all times? I like him, mind you, but I wouldn't tell him the things I tell you. Honest, I wouldn't. Where did I stop? Do you remember, George?'

'Something about the cinema,' he said.

'Yes, we were in the cinema, weren't we? Well, I was never more surprised, I can tell you. When I touched him, it seemed to change him. He became just the reverse of his usual: there was no Mr. Shy-and-reserved about him then. I had to hold him back or I don't know where he would have been. When the lights went up there was never such a sight. He was all red and his eyes shining like damsons, and he looked at me so hard I wanted to laugh. Then the lights went out and the next film was an educational; a silly thing about sunsets and apple trees in blossom. He didn't give a single glance to the film, but was just trying all the time to get an arm round me, and I, thinking he was going rather fast, just didn't understand, but sat very tightly back in my seat.'

'So you didn't let him get his arm round you?'

'No, I did not; the impertinence of him! I just gave him enough to keep him quiet, see. I took his hand and squeezed it, so that he couldn't get his arm around me. I kept hold of it so that he couldn't do anything. But when the big film, *Intolerance*, came on, he was another person. I might not have been there for all the notice he took of me, so much dust beneath his heel. You saw the film?'

ABOUT LEVY

'I remember the name,' he said, 'now you mention it, but I didn't go. I was very young then.'

'I keep forgetting you're such a kid, but it was all mixed up. It was five stories all in one, and you didn't know where or when you were except by the clothes. I couldn't pick it out at all, the sub-titles ran so fast I didn't have time to read them. But he went as cold as a block of ice, and it made me so angry I didn't know how to sit still in my seat.

'I'd never liked him, and it made me so wild that he should be one minute all over me and the next minute all eyes for a silly film. When we were out—it was dark then, and struck cold after the warmth inside—he called a taxi and took me back to the hospital. He didn't seem to know that he'd been doing anything queer, and turned his face on me all silly with pleasure; you know how the lights flap by. He didn't realise until I held myself back and wouldn't let him touch me. I kept him at a length until we were just getting to the hospital, and then I let him kiss me: but I wouldn't kiss him. It made me laugh to see him, that was so proud, buried on my neck and begging a kiss from my lips, which I wouldn't give him.'

'Why did you let him make love to you, if you didn't like him?'

He had got off the bed and was dressing. Now he stood in his shirt doing his tie up. A repulsion from her made him wish to get out into the streets.

ABOUT LEVY

She stretched her arms behind her head, laughing. She showed her big white teeth.

'You don't understand, George. That's why I like you. You're young, but that's a thing you'll never understand, not if you live to be a hundred. I don't know myself why I did it; it was just natural to me. You should have seen him after that evening. There was nothing he wouldn't do for me, and nothing in God's earth he wouldn't get; but nothing he could do was good enough for me. He must have spent a small fortune in treats, not counting presents besides. And when I told him I didn't love him, it seemed only to make him keener. He followed me about like a little dog; was a joke with the nurses.'

He put on his coat.

'Did he ask you to marry him?'

'Did he ask me? I should say so. Not once, but a dozen times. I never gave him a straight "no," because he was useful until I married Charlie. Then I told him just what I thought of him. I'd been wanting to for such a long time. It made me feel grand.'

'What did he do then?' George said.

'I never saw him again. But he sent us a wedding present. What d'you think it was?'

'I dunno. I'm going out.'

'Twin beds, all brass,' she said. 'Wasn't that nice?'

'Yes,' he said. 'So long. I shall get work to-day.'

'What work?'

ABOUT LEVY

'Some work somewhere. I don't care what I do. I must get work to-day.'

'Cheer up, George. You'll get it.'

Then, as he was going out, she said: 'You've forgotten something, George.'

He came back to her and bent down. She pulled down his head and kissed him on the cheek. He avoided her lips.

15.   Victor Levy was small and half-bald; wings rose above the ears, or grey horns of hair. His wife was younger, an auburn Jewess with subtle features.

He walked about the room; stopped, looking at a vase or table; then strode round again. All the time he talked, while she sat in an arm-chair listening.

'No, no. This boy is no damn good. His father was no good before him. He didn't believe in anything. I had to help him with money, and then he married a Christian on it. Even when he died, it was too late. The children were born, the harm had already been done. They didn't thrive, nor will their children after them. We took Ruth into our home and treated her as our own child. We gave her upbringing, love. Ach! we have spent all our duty on the girl. I made a good settlement on her and married her into the best Jewish family. She is rich, and she is happy.'

'Of course Ruth is happy. And it was you who made her so. But she was young when she came to us and

ABOUT LEVY

grew into our family. She is really one of us. But Claude has no idea of family; there's never been an opportunity before in which you could show what kinship means. If you don't do so now, you can't blame him for being ungrateful, because he won't have had anything to be grateful for.'

'I will not think of Claude; he is an atheist. He has forgotten his religion and his race and us. Why should we think of him? He thinks nothing of us. You are mad, my dear. Claude's *kaputt*—done for. We couldn't save him if we wanted to.'

'He must have money, Victor. It's expensive to be accused of murder in this country. Even if he's guilty he needs the money; if he's not, he deserves it.'

'If he's acquitted, he'll do what his father did—marry a Christian with my money.'

'That's his affair. He's Joseph's son and your nephew. You owe him a duty as that. Do you remember when he came to us after he had left school, that school where they tried to make him a parson? I talked with him then. He said he felt lost, not only that he had lost his father and mother, but all grip and hold.'

'Well, I agreed with him!'

'But he tried to find himself in us. That's why he came to see us. He thought we had what he had lost.'

'But he found nothing. Can a eunuch find manhood?'

'No, Victor. That's not fair. He didn't want cleverness—he had enough of that for himself—but some firm simple belief he could trust. Well, there was Ruth, who is not very deep. All she wants is money and safety, and now her husband and children satisfy her completely. Then he met us, and we couldn't give him what he wanted. We didn't try; but if we had had what he wanted he could have taken it without our trying. The whole of our way of thinking was alien to his upbringing. The person he found among us who has helped him most is Miriam.'

'No, I say. I say he's a disbeliever.'

'Not necessarily wicked, though.'

'That bears no weight with me.'

'But a member of the family of which you're the head.'

'Oh, I'll give him the money. But will he take it?'

16. Colonel Hall strode through the open gate and came on the men by the side of the hedge. They were lying at the foot of an oak eating bread and cheese. A dapple of light thrust through moving leaves broke over the grass and their slack bodies. When they saw the Colonel, they braced themselves. Johnson, the head man, jerked himself up, his mouth still full of food, looked round at the men and walked over, screening them.

'Morning, sir.'

'What's this mean?' The Colonel's face was even whiter than usual, his lips straight, bloodless and thin.

'The men are having their dinner, sir.'

'I can see that. Why the devil have they stopped for it? That's what I want to know.'

'They always have done, sir.'

'Well, don't let them in future. They can perfectly well eat it while they're working. How do they think you're going to get the hay in at this

ABOUT LEVY

rate. It's fine enough now, but it'll rain before night.'

The men had got up and were returning to work. They didn't speak. One kicked a stone and lifted it into the hedge.

'You lost nearly half the crop last year through idling.'

Johnson stood silent.

'I've never heard such nonsense as stopping for lunch. You'll be bringing picnic-baskets out here next.'

Johnson put on his cap, but did not move.

'What are you standing there for now?'

'I wanted to say on behalf of myself and the men that we are very sorry about Mr. Christopher,' Johnson said.

'Sorry. Keep your sorrow for yourselves. God knows you'll need it before the harvest's out, if you go on as you are going. He got what he deserved.'

Johnson walked off to the carts.

The Colonel stood watching till he had resumed work. 'Sorry,' he kept saying. 'To be poisoned by a dirty little Jewish doctor. Sorry! Damn good riddance, I say.'

Then he continued the round of the farm, striking heads off thistles and nettles.

17. 'THE accused, in admitting so much, gave evidence of a desire to help the trial and clear himself of the charge. He might have been silent had he wished. His account of what happened is intelligible; however remarkable it may seem that one man should take charge of another's conduct of life to the extent that, as a result of his bullying, the man he was trying to help should commit suicide. Whether such an action, however well intentioned, is morally reprehensible or not is not the question for us. There is no legal apparatus by which a man can be condemned for acting as he says that he has. So that if you accept the account given by the accused, your duty is plain to return a verdict of not guilty.

'But before you decide in favour of the accused, you must consider first the motives adduced by the prosecution for murder; and then certain facts which might seem to tell against the veracity of the accused's account.

'Miss Mason stated in evidence that she had been

ABOUT LEVY

used to visit the accused on Sunday afternoons to take tea with him. His conversation interested her, and she liked talking with him. He appears to have had a similar ascendancy over her to that which he had over the deceased. She used to ask his advice and often to be ruled by it. You have seen Miss Mason in the witness-box, and you will remember that on the conclusion of her evidence I had occasion to thank and congratulate her for the frank, straightforward way in which she had answered the questions put to her; questions which, from their nature, must have been extremely painful to her. We may assume that Miss Mason's evidence is not in dispute, with the exception of one piece of evidence to which I will refer later. Miss Mason said that when Hall made her an offer of marriage, she did not give her answer immediately, but went to consult the accused. This is a remarkable sign of the accused's power! She did not consult her mother, but a stranger. For a girl of Miss Mason's self-reliance to prefer the accused's opinion to her mother's or her own, shows that at this time at any rate his judgment commanded her respect. When she had placed the position before him, the accused strongly advised her not to marry Hall, whom he had known considerably longer than Miss Mason, and whom he did not consider a fit husband for her. She asked for reasons, and he gave several, such as might be expected from his knowledge of the deceased. Miss

ABOUT LEVY

Mason declared that she knew all these reasons for not marrying Hall, but that she thought she might marry him nevertheless, because he was not wholly bad if you knew him. The conversation grew heated; neither party seems to have considered carefully what was said, and at the conclusion of the argument the accused begged Miss Mason to come and see him again before she gave any answer to Hall.

'She went next day to the accused's flat, and as soon as he opened the door she noticed that he was excited. She made no comment, as she herself was feeling nervous, and the accused's manner, though unusual for him—did not seem so unusual considering the interest he took in her proposed step. When she had sat down, she told him that she had decided to accept the deceased's proposal of marriage. The accused said that he had been afraid she would; and then to her surprise explained that the reason of his disapproval had been partly because he wished to marry her himself. He asked her not to marry Hall, but him. He was very earnest and passionate in his declaration. He said he had not spoken before because he was so much older than she: and had not realised that she thought of marrying yet. But the thought of losing her—and to such a man—now made him speak. He could not live without her, and so forth.

'This sudden proposal greatly disturbed Miss Mason. She had never regarded the accused as a potential husband, but had looked on him as a disinterested person whose advice she respected. It is not difficult to understand the shock given to her feelings by this declaration, if she regarded marriage with the accused, as she said, repellent. But she did not leave the house at once, as might have been expected; she remained to explain that she did not reciprocate his feelings.

'The accused admitted the accuracy of Miss Mason's statement, but explained his conduct according to a very different motive. Miss Mason had not surprised him when she said that the deceased had asked her to marry him; but he was very surprised to hear that she thought of accepting. To him such a marriage appeared not unsuitable only, but disastrous. Miss Mason had not got the influence over the deceased that she thought she had. What influence she had was for evil, not for good. Hall, desiring to arouse her pity and her love, found that he could do so most easily by misbehaving and then asking her pardon. That was the only way in which the deceased could attract anybody's attention. Miss Mason's feelings towards the accused seemed mixed; she wanted a husband who would also be a son. He had not fully understood this at the first interview owing to words that she used then; she said in favour of marriage with Hall, "I want to be a married woman, I want to get away from home," and again, "I must marry soon." He realised now that these were not Miss

ABOUT LEVY

Mason's real motives for marrying Hall; she offered them merely as excuses. He asked her to come and see him before she gave her answer to Hall, because he hoped that she might have changed her mind, and because, if she hadn't, he intended to propose to her. He did not do so there and then, because he did not think of it until he was saying good-bye to her. He was at pains to explain to the court the state of mind in which he made the proposal. He had never before thought of asking Miss Mason to marry him. Though fond of her, he was not in love with her. If Miss Mason had not been about to decide on such an injudicious marriage, he would never have made the proposal. Marriage with Hall was bound to be a failure; he felt fondness was a secure foundation for marriage. He had failed through lack of insight; he was ashamed of this, but not of his action. When Miss Mason had said that she wanted to be a married woman, he should have realised that that motive was secondary to her desire to marry the deceased.

'This is a very extraordinary explanation, but no one will deny that it is ingenious. But then the accused is obviously a very ingenious man. You have to judge whether his ingenuity is directed to the solution of this young woman's problems or to clearing himself of the charge of murder. If his account is correct, he acted with almost incredible altruism. You may ask yourselves how many men would act with such altruism when making a proposal of marriage to a handsome young woman.

'The two accounts agree; with one exception. But that is a very important exception. The accused affirmed that Miss Mason had said that she wished to be a married woman. Miss Mason did not mention it in her evidence, and on being recalled utterly denied it. She was asked by counsel for the defence whether she remembered everything that she had said at that interview. She replied that she did not, but she remembered what she had not said; a statement that puzzled the defence but did not puzzle me, nor perhaps will it puzzle you, members of the jury. According to the account given by the accused, his proposal was made in a calculating state of mind; but with the appearance of passion, because he wished to persuade Miss Mason and thought that that was the only way to do so. In short, he declares that he was acting.

'The obvious implication of Miss Mason's evidence is that the accused had a motive for murder, to wit, jealousy. Before you can decide this, you must be certain in your minds whether the accused was sincere in his proposal or not. And you must bear in mind that the fact that Miss Mason thought that he was sincere is no evidence that he was. If you decide that the evidence of his sincerity is not sufficiently strong, you must consider the proposal to be as insincere as the accused maintains it was. If, on the other hand, you decide that the proposal was

ABOUT LEVY

sincere, you must not consider that the existence of jealousy as motive constitutes the commission of crime.

'A further motive proposed by the prosecution, either as alternative or concomitant to that of jealousy, is the desire, to which the accused admits, of wishing to prevent the marriage between Miss Mason and the deceased. You may think that without the additional motive of jealousy, this motive would carry little weight with the accused; or, again, you may think that a man, whose altruism extended as far as the accused claims that his did, might extend it even to the commission of murder.

'The court will now be adjourned for lunch and meet again at half-past two, when I will conclude my summing up.'

18. Miriam left the house without Janet calling her. Though it was shortly before lunch, she could not bear to think of eating with her; nor of the tortuous allusions she would make in order that the maid might not understand. Looking up at a front window, as she clicked the garden gate to, she saw Janet's face beside the drawn curtain. Neither made sign, and Miriam stepped into the shelter of the wall, where Janet could no longer see her.

Strong sun sparkled on the concrete paving, starring knobs of flint, to the eyes dazzling, hot to the feet. Plane trees slanted clusters of shade into the gutter and near roadside. 'Stop me and buy one' stopped in a cool coin, sometimes ringing his bell, mostly clinging to the iron rail with mahogany hands.

She passed from this road into the older one that ran up past 'The Spaniards.' She had a short lunch there. It was a week-day and the place was deserted. She had never been there except with Claude. To her it was his place, formed with his concept of it. Though memory of him crowded back into her,

ABOUT LEVY

it did not bring any illusion that he was present; made her more conscious than ever of his absence. He might never be there again: his place would continue and be other people's place; but he wouldn't come back. He really might be condemned. Janet had just buried him, with her words.

She couldn't eat any more. She called the waiter and paid. Blood was quickening in her arteries. She felt strong force in arms and legs. Her body was intent to help. She was walking on the trod earth between bushes. It comforted her to know that her body was so strong and willing. Then, as this strength weakened, the knowledge that her mind had been suppressing broke through into consciousness. Her will was useless to help against the law. Physical power could not overcome police force. She sat down on a seat, weak and sweating.

There were three men teaching coursers to race. Jack and Fred and Bert called to Queenie, Flossie and Roy. The high-flanked dogs bounded back to their masters and jumped at them. They swore the dogs down and held them straining. Then, the catch slipped, the dogs leapt again from the leash; Queenie, the mother bitch, lengthening to the fore, her head and barrel almost in the same line horizontal to the ground; the other two yapping at her flanks. All time the men cried encouragement, knit with their dogs' speed.

She got up and walked off: the absorbed men had not noticed her. She walked slowly away; the fire

ABOUT LEVY

dead within her and the sun's flame burning and consuming her energy utterly. Slowly through the bushes, clinging to shade; past a tramp stretched as if crucified stiff; across the road, high cambered like the top of a great pipe, the tar glistening like new skin. Down into Ken Wood.

Claude might have been dead; for her thought was always in the past. There was no future. The place was thick with times; his thought fell in shadows on the paths. His initials were on the bridge, where he had idly scratched them on the stone this spring. His hand, holding a latch-key, scratched them as he talked, and the marks remained, C. L., though duller than before. Winter would cover them. There would be no sign next spring. His thoughts were still present, but their occasions spent. He had been over this place with her, and the sayings remained like a salt deposit, when his tide had receded. He had gone from this place.

Thought of him quietened her; for her he was not a troubling person. His world was a moving world, but flowed steadily changing by its banks. It could not be blocked for long or diverted. He was no torrent, spate, or dry rocky bed for walking, but broad, with a solid onflow. This had borne her; she was not a rider of rapids. Before she had met him her life had been brackish and stagnant; but, after, it was as if the gate had been lifted and she moved out with him along his course with the same even motion. And now it was as if his flowing were ended, the stream turned in at a fissure in the rock and was gone; and she was diverted into some backwater. There was the old stagnancy, the pond film settling, yet still a fret of flowing beneath.

'You know a gyroscope,' he said, 'spinning and moving along a string of its own power. Seeing it, you wonder how it can move or remain, independent of its circumstance. To me, that thing poised at an angle, defeating the laws of gravity, is a marvel. Yet it's what I'm trying to do. To be apart from the practical world and philosophise appeals to me. But I can't do it. Not in a world of want and suffering. Even if I get away from the sight of it, there is still its memory, and I can't avoid that. I've got to preserve the insight of a philosopher in the complexity of phenomenal life; to see the world in the grain of sand ; and not to preserve insight only, but act on it and not get flustered. That can only be done by being emotionally as independent of people as a gyroscope is of gravity.' I said, *'But a gyroscope has got to have somebody to set it going.'* *'You pull the string in me,'* he said—oh, his smile and playing hands—*'you set me going. You are the beginning and the end of the process. I should be useless without you.'*

She looked down at the strewn mass of London in heat, towards somewhere where he was in court.

What does he matter to these millions? Who cares about his life? The great spread of buildings, the press of people, their blind pushing and number, overwhelmed her. His stature was nothing to their mass and weight. *One ant among five million struggling*

ABOUT LEVY

peltering ants raises itself and says, 'I am head and shoulders taller than any of the five million ants here.' Oh yeh? Mass and weight counted, the dead weight of mass. The city gave up the heat of its millions and repelled her with its chaos. Yet its plate of gold-dusted roofs rising to spire and dome frightened her with sublimity. She was not on a hill, looking down at it; but it rose, a gold lake, to draw her into its depth, where mud was, and slime. Its surface was vast, beating up the sun. But underneath it was foul with all decay; when it was probed, would give forth marsh gas; stirred, the black strands of corruption would rise into the clear.

She was standing outside, alone on a hill, looking down on the glimmering of sun upon the roofs. But he was in the depth covered in the gloom of court. She looked down into the gleam, but it struck up at her, opaque.

She did not feel now the blank loss, the doubt of the ended path, or trembling before the hole in the rock, through which his life flowed, parting from hers. But she felt now the old pain of being with him. For though they had seemed to flow together steadily, she had always been dragging on him in a slower motion. It was like the stairs of a moving stairway and the travelling leather belt. Perhaps they travelled at the same speed, but the belt was on the outside and had farther to go; when they were linked, the stairs pulled on and the leather lagged always and could go no faster.

ABOUT LEVY

She wanted the link of being joined to him physically, and not always to travel around and parallel with him. Even when she had given up hope and thought of marriage, she wanted to be able to stretch out her hand and touch so that she could be sure that he was there and the whole motion was not illusion. But when she wanted to touch him and place herself where their flesh could meet, he was off arcing to her parallel.

It was always like this, except once soon after she had met him. Then suddenly his hand touched her neck; the electricity of his body charged her and poured from his hand through her body, fusing and burning her out. The hand passed round her neck, feeling and knowing the bones and flesh of the neck with fingers. The hand went on with parted fingers into her hair, delicately feeling the skin and the hair and the roots of the hair; feeling the bones even of the skull and giving always the tingling stimulus out in touch.

Then she looked into his eyes, which were pupilled to hard jet, so that no depth was in their circle, only a forward-raying. She saw her face in them as in two small glasses; that was their depth, the perspective of what was reflected in them. The pupils had contracted to black stones, and now all smoothness flaked from his face, the skin drawn tight across his bones.

Still as she looked, their bodies not touching, his hand linked them with his arm. She, watching him, was at once terrified and attracted. She was terrified by the new element in him of shrivelled hardness, yet was drawn towards him because she knew what he was and he was still recognisable. Half of him was a new force of blind impulse, urgent yet impersonal; half of him human, yet away from her. He was split; his inhuman part came at her; his other part, which she knew, stood away, watching. She was afraid of the new self which was coming to her, yet persisted to come at the self which was aloof. She wanted to brush away the first blind onset and fraternise with the reinforcements.

Yet she thought now perhaps he had seen the same division in her. For it was her lips that came forward, it was her half-parted mouth that sought the contact; and her mind was aloof as his was, waiting the storm's cease. Her mind was apart, but stretching forward towards the meeting, like eyes in a fog. But his mind was averted, blinded by the smoke of the striving self. She could go through it; but he had to turn away till it was all over.

Then he met her ready lips with his mouth. Everything was rigid still, except his straying hand and their slow lips. As the pressure tautened, his body and hers bent and fitted, clamping and clamped into one being. His hands viced her body, and she bound the unity together with her hands about him. With the pressure of his mouth towards her, her head swung back to accept it and her loins swept in a curve into his hips. Each part and place of their two bodies was fitted and welded in this

ABOUT LEVY

embrace; minds forgotten, his force met hers, joining along it.

His braced body grew limp. His stretched body went dead suddenly; she held dead weight in her arms. His head, collapsed, lay on her shoulder.

She did not know what to do. It was as if, while holding a stick of solder, she saw it bend and fall and melt before no flame. His head lay on her shoulder, and she held him with difficulty, plunged from ecstasy into ridicule. She got him to a chair and sat beside him on the arm. He sat crumpled like a top-heavy sack, his head dropped in his arm and resting on her thigh. She never knew what he was doing then; thought he was crying, but there was no sound. No sound but her own voice, which said, 'What's the matter, Claude? Can I get you anything?' Then silence.

He raised his head in a moment. She could see no sign of tears; she was sorry she could see no sign of tears. She wouldn't speak before he spoke; and, before he spoke, he got up to go. All he said was in a steady voice. She would have liked it broken with emotion; wanted the shutters open for a moment; then would have helped to close them.

All he said was, 'Forgive me. I must go.'

'Why must you go?' she said. 'What is there to forgive?'

Saying this, she opened her eyes too wide. It was not what he had done, but how that had to be forgiven.

ABOUT LEVY

His hat was lying on a table. He took and crammed it on his head before he left the room. Then he took it off again.

He said good-bye, making for the door. He supported himself with his hands up either side the lintel.

'When shall I see you again?'

He said 'Sometime,' and left.

It was some time. She had to write to him three times before she got an answer. Then it was vague. He would come and see her soon. Soon meant a week more, and when he came, he was just as he had been before all this had happened. Just as aloof—as much himself. She did not refer to it then. She took the situation as he made it.

Later, when she tried to talk of it, all he said was, 'No, it's no good. I know it's no good. I'm not made that way, and for me to try is silly.' He would go no further, however much she pressed him to be more definite. He would explain and talk of anything else; but this remained an unexplained corner of himself.

So they continued in their parallel course; now he was always aloof; she always trying to touch and awake the impersonal self, to equate it with the self she knew.

It was getting late. She turned towards Hampstead.

19. The table on which the bowl stood was shrivelled away in light so that its colour and texture changed to the eye. The surface kept going up into rays about the bowl edge. A coin, too, of light was in the bottom of the bowl. Table and bowl were caught from their being into a process of apparent dissolution and melted into life.

The hot china gave no satisfaction even to the touch. It had been chill, the restoring cool of shade. Now it was hot, not with a withdrawn warmth of its own, but with the sun's heat. It had lost its secret separate beauty and taken itself into the disturbing hot moving beauty of life: this did not resemble her life. Hers moved like an engine, driven by her husband's power, a circular route along lines with no terminus. She would go round and round until she stopped; then a holiday, before, wound up, she took the lines again. And finally, when something broke, the scrapyard.

Not her life, but the life of veering air in leaves shaking the drops down; of light like milk, hunting

ABOUT LEVY

shadows on cool streams; of the hot sun warming and piercing spawn in shallow ponds, the black specks growing in jelly-cradles cupped in submerged hoof-marks; of the ever-altering strain of weather; of wrestlers; the resisting yet retiring branches; of the thrust of the grass to the air; of the stallion and the ram; the body bent forward to the thrusting arm and sword. The life of dazzling colours, of curves, of the looping 'plane; the hands of a dancer, a swan's wings in flight, night wind across a hole.

The table was caught into this life, the bowl was; but Ruth remained outside.

She remained outside; she could not enter after her bowl for fear of the dazzling multitude of other things that would surround her. She knew she could go in, but she didn't dare to.

Claude was in this world when they met again in London. She was not at ease with him. His mind moved too fast about her, and knew her utterly at first meeting. There was nothing she could say or do that was new to him or surprised him. Victor and Irène didn't demand novelty or surprise. All the people she knew distrusted it. He attracted her by quickness of thought and movement, and at the same time upset her. She wanted to break out in some way in response, but she didn't know the way. To want him was to want annihilation. She was a twig on a bush that waved and scratched, fixed in space: he flowed, a river beneath. She was conscious of his determined power and passage. She wanted to be like him, but

ABOUT LEVY

knew that if she fell she would lose certainty; and even then not be like him, but a twig, without force of its own, carried on the flood of his power.

So that she turned away from him, seeing the danger of his influence. She spoke against him slyly. She mined his faults as a rich quarry. He was so serious: he had no sense of humour—yet his wit was round and bound her. He was shy about women and not worldly wise. He, who appeared so sensible, was a fool about money; anyone could take him in with a story of want or failure. He did not know how to spend nor get the best from it. He might have bought furniture and pictures and all sorts of beautiful things. But he continued to live in digs in a mess, giving to fools and knaves and failures: while she had known until her marriage that she could have borrowed from him; but she had pride, and he would not give to any who did not ask. Yes, really, he bought up pride in the cheapest market.

They did not often meet. There was no will to on either side. Each felt that the blood relation must mean something, something normal and solid. Yet to him there was only indifference: to her at first this attraction and then hatred. Not admitted as hatred, but indulgent, piercing hate.

Yet still a part of her was his. This part went traitor to her solid, static self. It believed that he was right, yet wished to capture him and bind him down helpless; to hold him up, the bush damming the river,

ABOUT LEVY

the twig zigging in the current. So that she 'phoned him sometimes suddenly to come to dinner, in imagination seeing him cramped into her life. Then she found him as before, moving with the same power, and for the moment wished to be taken with him: and, when he was gone, made fun of him.

Now more terrifying was the evanescence of bowl and table into changing life; because Claude, core and cause of such desire of living, was on trial. They summoned her to this beauty and the court. Such men ended there.

Ended there—but the bowl was still the inviting stage of such tragedy. It was a play she could act in dream. It would be real, yet real only at the moment of its action. She was the queen cast in the sea in a chest, her children with her. She floated the waves, the invisible current to a new land, and, when she landed, everything was different. It was this earth still, but each speck seemed changed because she was queen now—queen-mother without the tyrant husband. He was beyond the last wave seen, and she was queen among her children, and the new people received her. The sons grew up to avenge her wrongs. They picked crews of men, and rowed singing out from the harbour. They would return victorious.

A hand rapped on the door. The bowl, still in the same light, did not seem to change. The world set firm. The safety curtain was lowered. She walked to the door.

20.   AFTER the speeches there was lunch in the drill hall. The horses had been pulled back, the ropes taken down and coiled, the spring-boards stacked, and Hill sat at the high table. He, chaplain before last, sat between the ex-headmaster and his wife, and while the choir sang grace in the gallery behind his head, looked down the rows of present Rockleyans and their parents. He saw, among the ranks of bent heads like sunflowers, the long-distant faces of men whom he had known as boys, faces lined with worry, paternity, poverty and lust, or grown sleek and coarsened by affluent indulgence. Here and there was a face like Common's, burned and conditioned by hard physical life. That was the type he liked; men who could box and run, men who could hit a six. He did not like rugger players much, because he had never been able to play the game well himself.

Scrumble shamble and they all sat down. Talking broke through the heat and religious air. A horde of harridans poured from a door, bearing soup. It was

ABOUT LEVY

always soup. When it was cold, everybody said, 'Soup! What a good idea.' To-day it was hot.

'No soup for me, thank you,' Father Hill said.

Claude, when he was a boy, didn't sit near me, because I've always sat at the high table; he used to sit with Diddlum's people; she must have been pretty once. Old Common was a man, looked like a soldier; though he was in Oil. Organised that special constabulary marvellously during the war. If there'd been any airraids or spies, they'd 've had a poor time with old Common around. Esther Levy did a lot of work for the parish, when she came back. Really it was she put the W.I. on its legs. Could manage things; but had no way with children. I did something to discipline them; but the mischief had already been done. Remember how upset she was that she'd beaten Claude for burning those clothes or whatever they were. Ah, salmon, that's better.

They gave him a larger helping because he had had no soup. Blubber, the ex-headmaster, said that was the reward of abstinence. Hill laughed; his wife smiled because her husband had made a joke.

Blubber said, 'You make up on the fish what you lose on the . . . what was the last course?'

They laughed—a he's-just-the-same-as-ever laugh. Blubber had been a great headmaster. The great thing about him was he never could remember anything. He once put his top-hat on his hand and his gloves on his head. This was characteristic— what one expected of old Blubber—and people loved him for it.

ABOUT LEVY

Look out for bones. And I once thought he would be a priest, who is now in the dock for murder. They lie in beds made for them, with a sort of salt deposit in this Canadian stuff. But I didn't think he would after that evening he spoke to me; as if I had been trying to force him! It was extraordinary the way he gave everything a personal twist. When I was only saying that there was no happier life than that of a priest. Very neurotic and introspective.

The maid knew him—he was an old friend; she had been serving as long as he had been eating these meals. He got a good helping of chicken and ham, and the salad was really nice.

He said to Blubber, 'I agree when they say you can't fast spiritually and physically at the same time.'

Blubber said, 'If you chew long enough, you can eat anything.'

'A poor fellow in my parish,' Hill said, 'fed on leather for three days. He said when it was boiled and chewed a hundred and sixty times it was quite edible.'

'Yees, yees, I should think it was,' Blubber said. 'Have some more peas; you've hardly got any.'

Hill helped himself. *He lost his way; and so he came a cropper.*

The heat shimmered on the grass outside. The cricketers had left to change. Boys in their black clothes were sweating, elbow to elbow, and gulping down the claret cup from their tiny glasses. Parents were shifting uneasily, wanting to smoke or get out, or both. But there was coffee; everyone had to wait for coffee, except the cricketers; no one dared not to. Parents were on their best behaviour; the whisky-swillers and toss-pots sipped lemonade down and took bread that the masters offered them.

Common's face was still very handsome; he was the only man who looked cool. The bones showed marks, forming the cheek and chin and skull. Hill thought, clean-limbed: but Common, happening to turn to high table, showed his eyes to be dark and disturbingly aloof. His power was not from hard muscle or the fleet foot; though he had these. It issued through eyes from the gleaming mind and hard, crystalline will. Common's eyes fixed into Hill's. Hill smiled; this look made him feel weak. But the smile did not turn the challenge off. Common might not be seeing him at all. The focus of his eyes was not on Hill's face, but beyond it; either right beyond it, looking through him like glass, or behind the face focused on the brain, piercing the flesh like a ray. *Too serious, he said, to be a priest, too serious. Too certain rather, too life-proud, too self-centred. Let him wait for age, wait till the sap goes dry and the arteries harden. He doesn't budget for weakness. What does he know of the clot and the stone? What counsel for cancer? Lo, I am who am weak, am made strong with the strength of Lord God.*

That look he had then was the same look that Claude gave him when he broke out against priests.

ABOUT LEVY

Yet they hadn't seen one another for years, who still had the same look.

I suspected that friendship; was wise to give Bubb a clue. Noticed this morning that he took the credit of having seen it to himself. I could believe it of Claude, but I don't know about Diddlums. He was so tidy and compact, always tucked away into himself, except towards Claude. That was so queer; Claude wasn't demonstrative about it—didn't give himself away at all. Yet I should have suspected that the enthusiasm would have been on his side. Perhaps was on his guard against me. Secretive always. Bubb's talk did all the good in the world; they didn't see nearly so much of one another. Though I kept in touch with Diddlums, of course, to help him if necessary. Rather marvellous the way I've been the friend of the school and so many wonderful boys all this time.

Coffee was finished and the benediction said. The chairs scraped back, a form fell. They filed out with a slow lollop of shoulders. Into the sun and on the crying grass. Groups and couples breaking and joining like bubbles on water: impulsive cries of recognition: remembered joy igniting like a match, a burst, a short, quivering flame. 'Have you seen Jenkins lately?' 'No.' 'But you were so intimate with him.' 'I met Jones the other day, Noël Jones, Captain of Fives in '21. He's in Standard Oil, doing well.' 'Noël Jones, which was he? I've forgotten him, but I remember the name distinctly.' A silence. So long.' 'Glad to have seen you.' Matchhead

ABOUT LEVY

gone grey, the shaft turning up and crackling: the charred wood dropped. Remembered—the racing losses, the furniture instalment unpaid for, Mabel sitting in the car because she's so shy, that confounded maintenance order.

Hill bounced unquietly before the pavilion: one hand raised always in greeting, the other in farewell; a filing in a field of magnets. He would usually have loved to be so distracted; but to-day he felt drawn against his will towards Diddlums. But Common was talking to Strumer; the Fabian and doctrinaire atheist, who had come as temporary master. He had been going in for law, but had to work while he did so. Took his examinations at a leisurely speed; but in five years he was ready to leave. That was sixteen years ago. Nothing external prevented him but he couldn't leave. Then he married a Czech woman whom he had met in Samos, inherited some money and bought an old stone cottage in the hills four miles off. He still talked of leaving; or rather, what he would do if he left. But he could not escape from interest in what the boys were doing. Though he pretended to be apart, their growth and experimentation, their uncontrolled energy, held him. He would never go from where he was supreme to a lower position in a higher place—a cock crowing on a dunghill, loving and despising his small kingdom. The wife never came to the school; but would entertain boys to tea at their house in the hills. Some of the

ABOUT LEVY

elder boys stayed for week-ends with them in the holidays. There were books and pictures there; sometimes a shabby celebrity. He was like no other master, a spend-force ranging his library and taking boys' thoughts to plump them. When he gave them back these ideas, they had grown so ambitious that the boys were often frightened. He realised himself only in boys. His son ran a short riot through Oxford and Bolivia and was killed in a car smash. Strumer was a failed person, but an energiser; and so a good educator. Because he fulfilled a function which no one else on the staff could, he was kept on, despite his views. He kept on because he couldn't leave off.

Hill knew they were talking about Claude, even before he got near enough to overhear what Strumer was saying.

'He's the best thing this place has turned out since I've been here. That phrase "turn out" always amuses me; they say the public schools turn out the best boys. It's true; they only keep the worst, a survival of the unfittest. You remember Claude in that last term. Well, he was only seventeen and a half; could have stayed on another year if he'd liked, and I believe wouldn't have minded doing so. But they wouldn't let him because he was pacifist.'

'The year I was C.S.M. he was the only person who was not in the corps. Do you remember the debate?'

'Yes, that was what did it. I'm afraid I was

ABOUT LEVY

responsible for it. He was excellent; I was going to say for his age, but for any age he was very good. He just flailed them, including old Langtry, who was running the corps. The way he held the mirror of their own religion up to those Christians made my heart warm. The fact that he was half-Jew made it more subtle.'

'If you remember, I seconded him. There was a fuss about it afterwards, wasn't there?'

'Yes, the fact that you were C.S.M. made it worse. They refused to publish an account of it in the *Rockleyan* and 'the Blubber' spoke to me about choosing less controversial subjects.'

'And was that why he left?'

'Yes, we had a lovely house-masters' meeting about it. You remember I was his house-master. Four of the house-masters besides myself were fit to join up themselves; but that didn't make any difference. They all made patriotic speeches, and I asked them why they didn't join up if they felt like that. Actually Sargent did join up after that; and was killed in his first month out there. But the meeting broke up in disorder; they wanted my blood and Claude's. I expected that they'd demand my resignation, but Blubber said he'd deal with the matter himself. All that happened, was that Claude didn't come back next term.'

'He never told me. I shouldn't have expected him to keep that sort of silence.'

The cricketers came out, laughing and throwing

ABOUT LEVY

the ball from one to another. Old Langtry, who hadn't played for fifteen years because of his lumbago, walked out with the professional to umpire. They called Langtry 'Gus.' It was not short for Augustus or Gustave; it had just grown naturally on him like the hair in his ears. His skin was like wrinkled parchment. He loved birds. He always umpired this match, white-coated beneath the sweaters—a shapeless mass of hidden sensibility.

Common saw Hill droning back and forward about to alight on them, but he turned away and faced the pitch. Then he said, 'One of my most vivid memories of Claude was in common-room. I went there this morning during speeches; and though the room's now painted ox-blood instead of the old dung colour, and there's a wireless, it recalled the whole thing clearly to me.'

'Yes, ox-blood shoulder high and mustard above with a dark line between to prevent their clashing; the separation of two incompatibles by a third incompatible.'

'Claude used to pronounce his name "Lev-y." He was very ashamed to have a Jewish name in a Christian school. The boys all used to call him Levi or Ikey. For a time it infuriated him, so that he was quite popular; but as he grew out of it they began to dislike him more and more, as they couldn't rag him. Besides, he was much more intelligent than they were, and for that, too, they hated him. Again your elimination of the fittest. What I remember so clearly, was standing on the edge of a group of small boys—it was about the end of my second term—watching some older boys kick Claude round the room. He was rolled up in a sort of ball, with his arms knit to protect his head. I didn't understand why they were doing it, and I was sorry for him; but I thought that as they were older he must deserve it; and I was pleased too. It gave me a sort of satisfaction, even his white face and the blood coming from his nose, and his wanting to cry and not doing so. Then they went away—I suppose they didn't like remaining in the room with a person they had treated in that way. I and the younger ones left behind wouldn't touch him or speak to him or brush him. We sat pretending to read books till he went out too; then we were relieved, and none of us spoke of it. We were probably ashamed that we thought it strange or brutal.'

'Was this before I came?'

'You had just come, I think. You hadn't taken over the house then. It was still under Dawson.'

Father Hill stood by them. 'Exchanging the odd reminiscence?' he said. 'How Strumer talks when you give him the chance. You can tell me, Strumer: that's Witherspoon and Jollyboys in now, isn't it? Is this Witherspoon any relation of Harry Witherspoon who was here a few years ago? Must have left in '23, and nearly got his rowing blue at Cambridge.'

'I never thought to ask,' Strumer said. 'Perhaps he's a bastard by one of the maids.'

ABOUT LEVY

He turned away, nodding to Common. 'I shall see you later.'

'Dear Strumer,' Father Hill said, 'was so refreshing—when he first came.' He took Common by the arm and said, 'You know, I've scarcely seen you to-day; I've been so busy. But I'ld like a few words with you, if you can spare a moment.'

Common's arm hung as if it had been shot in the shoulder: Hill let it go. They walked side by side over the grass, Common looking down at his shoes and the priest's black boots, which were wrinkled beneath the toecaps like worried faces. They walked round behind seated parents and boys lying on the grass at their feet.

Hill had two voices, one loud and hearty, with which he cried, 'Oh, good shot, sir,' so that everybody looked round and then clapped, or 'Hallo, Tony,' when the parents would ask who he was; the other low, spoken from the corner of his mouth so that people could not hear, a distorted and husky confidence.

These he used as the occasion demanded, speaking to Common softly.

'I feel you want an explanation about Claude. You feel that I haven't done my duty.'

'What makes you think that?'

Hill paused, then said, 'I saw it from your eyes.' Then loudly, 'Oh, good catch; did you see? Mid-on falling forward went for it with his right and caught it with his left. It must be Douglas who did that.'

ABOUT LEVY

'My eyes? Why should they blame you? I don't know what you could have done.'

Hill did not speak. He tried to take Common's arm again, but Common was swinging it. He saw the lines of the boy's face he had known and imposed himself on, but now drawn to a man's face away from him. He dropped his hand.

I pity you, Diddlums; you've got such a hard face.

Common said: 'You were such an unsuitable pair; you were so far apart that there was nothing you could give each other. Even common sympathy was almost impossible.'

'It wasn't my fault,' Hill said. 'I didn't want to adopt him. His mother asked me on her death-bed to be his guardian, and I agreed for her sake. My home, wherever it was, was always open to him. He cut away the bond and refused to visit me. When I wrote to him he didn't answer. You must remember, too, that my guardianship ended when he was twenty-one. He hasn't been to see me since then.'

Jennings, the new batsman, strode out to the wicket with flapping pads.

'Jennings,' Hill said. 'You can always tell a Jennings because they all have knock-knees.' Softly, 'Of course, I'm terribly sorry for Claude.'

'Of course you are,' Common said. 'Anyone would be who knew him. Even to people reading the case, sympathy must be on his side.'

'Yet I think I'm being weak. I think all this sympathising with murderers is weak.'

ABOUT LEVY

'It's not that here; it's not a general sympathy with murderers. As Strumer says, this case is peculiar. I was just going to tell you when you interrupted me. Popular sympathy will only be in his favour if he's guilty. People can't understand the defence he's put forward. But they can understand the prosecution. They could understand a person acting from such motives, and would sympathise with him.'

'But it's murder then,' Hill said. 'Oh, beautiful glide, clean between square and silly fine leg. He's young, that boy; one day he'll make a first-class cricketer. His father's Vicar of Sleedale; used to play for Durham County. A slow bowler with an incredible spin.'

He stood looking at the game; obviously, to the parents, appreciating it, a priest with energy and normal interests—a sport.

He said in his asiding voice: 'I'm terribly grieved about Claude; but there's nothing I can do.'

He turned.

Diddlums had disappeared.

Hill caught an eye, a small bright-faced boy's who was lying by his parents' chairs.

'Hullo, Roger,' he said. 'How are you? Been beaten lately?'

21.   She tried to rest her head in the corner of the cushions, but the taxi swerved and jolted and her head swung with it, but always a little farther, so that it was jerked back like weight on end of string. Plates, her eyelids, closed doors upon fires, her eyes. Then she was ready to die. She could not have held out her life for an angel to take. She had no will, even to die; not if it meant even as little as holding a ticket out to a collector and passing a barrier. She would lie as she did, jolted and bumped, in the midspace between life and death; all will and consciousness balanced, attracted but unmoved, in the between-part. She felt her mother's hand faintly, holding hers. It meant almost nothing—a fly buzzing round a sleeping dog. She squeezed back. But though the pressure continued, she did not notice it.

Mrs. Mason, a withered chrysanthemum in a rising wind, looked at her daughter taken into sorrow she could not share. Her skin was wrinkled pink verging to yellow, an apple's skin kept till

ABOUT LEVY

Christmas for the party. A little bruised in parts, but very sweet. She did not wish to be so much a fruit, so faded a flower. She wanted to enter her daughter's intimate life: to set glass in her daughter's skull to see the brain thinking, or be within her daughter's body, the jigger beneath the skin. When the hand squeezed back, it was contact between her alive half and the live part of Edith struggling to live. It was the mother's consolation, to become a treasured intimacy.

The taxi took a sudden corner. They swung together. She clasped Edith, breast to her breast; she held her body against Edith's body. The girl did not resist. Had given up tenure of her frame. Her mind had not left it or risen, but was drowned under spate of sorrow, a deadening unanalysed grief. It buried her beneath the force of its descent, as a body struggling but borne back by the flood from chute to hold; there was no end to its impact of small stinging blows, which severally blinded and together were burying her.

Mrs. Mason held, flesh and bone, her daughter with her arm, pulling her on to her breast and soothing with fingers, learning the trick anew. The fingers had lost practice, that touched and trained Mason's young neck to love.

She began a sort of cradle croon; the driver saw all in his mirror and heard this crooning. But the girl had gone beyond giving way; she was seized to sickness of spirit in a dark chamber. She could not analyse this grief, the reason of sickness. It was falling faintness and at the same time pressure of all existence on her, with the darkness and suffocation following. Grief had so grown that it had become physical pain, and besieged head and lax limbs.

Edith then spoke, saying, 'He ought not to have let it happen, anyway. He should have stopped him; why had he got the poison with him, if he didn't intend to do it, all that poison? Or when Chris took it, he should have treated him; after all, he's a doctor.'

Mrs. Mason said, 'Yes, yes, yes, yes, yes.' She said, 'Yes, yes, yes, yes.'

'It's mad to think that if someone takes poison, you can only just stand and watch him die in agony without doing anything to help. He'd barely taken it, he said, before he came back. I know how Claude sat; back in his chair, watching. He was never all there with you in a room, wouldn't give himself to anyone. Even when he proposed, he never laid himself right open to me; he seemed always tiptoe to spring backward. O God, God, why did you let Chris die? Why did you let the poison kill him?'

Now her body grew rigid and her head pressed blind on to her mother's shoulder. The hard knob-knot of the shoulder fitted into one eye-socket. Her head held the down pressure, tightening the lid on the eye. Soon the tautness was thrummed with sobbing. Played in tuneless grief. Her body was

ABOUT LEVY

string, pulled back and then released, vibrating and resonant; it was not the sound nor the player. They were outside her; she was the struck gut.

Mrs. Mason was a support; she shored up her daughter. It was her duty to sit in the taxi, firm and straight, giving her shoulder for her daughter to cry on. She had to remain outside and be still. Her dress would be spoilt; she could feel warm tears already soaking on to her skin. But she must sacrifice her dress and avoid a scene. The taxi had stopped in a traffic block. Some people walking by looked in, but they went on for politeness.

The taxi-driver could see it all in his mirror. He had grown tired of seeing people kissing in the back. Only two lots had cried: a pregnant girl from Russell Square, whom a fat chap with spectacles sent off to Victoria Station; and a man who had been run over, his arm and ribs smashed, and he was there before the ambulance.

Edith tried to speak in order to become mistress of herself. Her voice was wrung and broken by the plucking of sorrow playing on her.

'Chris said he wouldn't commit suicide. He swore he wouldn't.'

This voice was not any of her kind; her mother wished she would not speak. She tried to hush Edith's voice into silence, to stroke her to quietness with her unpractised hand, because she was more afraid of the sounds of the sorrow than the sorrow itself. She could not bear them.

ABOUT LEVY

Yet the voice continued, 'If one had to go, let them both go. Then the board's clear for a new game. Let others play seriously; it's their turn.'

If only she would turn her face; lift her head up and raise her eyes. All her mother could see was a smart little hat shaking, and heard nothing but this twisted voice. She tried to strain the chin into the light with her other hand. But the chin moved, eluding fingers; the head nuzzled again into her shoulder.

'How he loved me!' the voice said. 'You can't imagine what he told me, the things he said about me, when he was absolutely broken down and I raised him up.'

She knew what Charles had said to her at Teddington, the day they went on the river right up to Hampton Court, the wonderful things he had said in the maze. She had borne half her married life because she was certain they were true, and fretted the rest because she found they had been only half true at the time and were now no longer true at all. Not after Trouville.

Mrs. Mason was glad: because she was no longer troubled by Charles; because Chris was dead; because Claude was going to be hanged; because Edith was resting on her shoulder, was helpless and shaken with grief and needed her.

She was sorrowful: because she knew that the moment was going to pass when she was needed. That she was but Alpha and Omega, who wished to

ABOUT LEVY

be the whole alphabet. That in a month or year, soon, they would be as far apart as before and further. The body between her hand and shoulder would never be hers by any other right than having borne it.

Now they were coming near their home; now another taxi was drawing near theirs. It followed them, and the polite man, who had been so kind in Lyons', sat back in it, legs crossed, admiring his shoes of buckskin and their brown toecaps. He cleaned his nails with an orange-stick from his waistcoat pocket, then blew on them and polished them till they gleamed and he could see his face in them. He combed his hair in a little mirror of polished steel.

'We're nearly there,' Mrs. Mason said. 'You must pull yourself together, Edith.'

She was sorry that the journey was almost finished and the moment of intimacy passed.

The girl lifted up her head slowly; then wiped her face; and tears from her swollen eyes. But when she saw herself again in her glass, she looked so wretched that she began to cry again. She was so plain with sorrow. But soon she was painting her twitching lips and powdering the damp skin, ready to out-brave a world and look St. John's Wood in the face.

The taxi stopped. She got out first and stood, waiting for her mother. As he walked by, a young man looked at her. Then her mother got down and fumbled in her bag. Edith took the bag and paid the fare.

Mr. (Tommy) Bright, leaning forward, tapped

the glass. The driver stopped fifty yards down the road.

They went in.

'Ever shaken hands with a lucky man?' Mr. Bright said.

'Not as I know,' the driver said.

'Shake hands with me, then. And buy the wife a bunch of violets with my love.'

'A port and lemon's more like it,' the man said, and turned the car round.

'They'll be keeping me on after all or my name's not Tommy Bright,' Mr. Bright said, and gave his nails another polish.

22. They sat in chairs in the garden, drawn away from the road on the bare grass. The chair-shades cast cool only over the heads and torsos. The legs were cut on the chair-rests and burned by the sun. All others had retired to their bedrooms for siesta; but Mason and Mrs. Failey lay out on the lawn.

'Why should you wish to hear more?' he said. 'What does it matter to you, all this I've been saying? We all have our troubles; why should you have mine as well as your own?'

'I can bear them, Charles,' she said. 'It'll do you good to get it off your chest.'

She made him feel like a child, and very happy. He looked at her, wishing she were his wife. She wasn't handsome; had a strange face. The flesh seemed not to exist, only to be there to hold her eyes and mouth. The eyes were set wide apart, with big grey pupils. They had a quality of looking into him and seeing everything and not hurting. They healed by soothing, not cautery. The mouth was brightly rouged,

ABOUT LEVY

an ensign, a flower, a scarlet ribbon. Her teeth shone between the lips like ivories in a red case; like peas in a ripped pod, they seemed new, gleaming to meet their first light.

She leant back, slim-formed to the canvas, her thin arms forming a diamond about her head, ready to listen.

He felt loathing of himself and his life in hydro bars. He hated that he could have her here, but nowhere permanent; that unconsciously she urged him to leave for active life and yet stay here. He was mad with her.

She turned her eyes to him, wanting him to speak. He felt vulgar, and this strain mounted to show itself before her.

'When Edith was small,' he said, 'I couldn't stand her except when she was asleep. She was always crying out in her thin voice; a sort of bleating it was, that made me mad. But when she slept and her face was quiet, there was nothing more beautiful on earth. Then I was proud to be her father. I wanted to do everything for her that I and money could.'

She flinched at 'and money.'

'I've always trusted in money,' he said. 'I know it's not everything; but lack of it's everything. I come from a poor family. I've known hunger. Talk of goodness, talk of beauty to a hungry man, and he'll think you daft. And he'll be right.'

'Yes, that's true, I suppose.'

'When Edith grew up, she grew away from me.

ABOUT LEVY

I forced her away from me. I knew what I was doing. Her mother didn't teach her to despise me. I taught her that. You don't do that by your own behaviour. You do it by sending the kid to a good school. You know it as well as I do. It's a commonplace on the movies. I knew what I was doing perfectly well. I didn't expect her to respect me, and she doesn't. I brought her up to be a lady. It was a funny thing to do, but I don't complain. I educated her so that she grew so graceful and so pretty that whenever I saw her I wanted to stretch out my hand and stroke her. And I knew all the time I had her so genteel that she was ashamed of me, and I couldn't touch her now.'

Mrs. Failey was looking at him, understanding with her eyes' extraordinary sympathy, and Mason pitied himself, suddenly believing what he was saying. He couldn't go on speaking.

Then he remembered that it was the first time he had seen what he had been blindly doing; that his explanation was false with the desire for sympathy. Part of him wanted to lie on her bosom sobbing in this pretended nakedness of spirit; part to be a man before her, stripped utterly and without reserve. This he surrendered to.

'No, I'm quite wrong,' he said. 'That wasn't right.'

She saw his figure cut clean-clear in a self-sacrifice.

'No, that was the right thing to do,' she said. 'I admire that.'

ABOUT LEVY

She wanted his self-creating explanation. That was drama.

'It was a fool thing to do.'

He meant to strip and be clean to the bare flesh and nervous motive. But he didn't know what of himself was real and what not. He was meshed before her, who demanded truth despite herself. She would take trash for treasure, turning it reverently in her white freckled hands. But he couldn't give it. Who had deceived himself lifelong, could not deceive her; and had nothing to offer but deception.

'God!' he said.

'What's the matter?'

'I don't know what's the matter.' Even now he expected that his voice should change and be rounded to toll bell-like for his lost integrity; but it was rough still with smoking and drink, a file or cat's tongue. 'I feel I've got to tell you what's wrong; but I don't know what's wrong, myself.'

Instantly her hand was on his, patting and pressing his hand down, soothing the striving in him, and beat his frenzy into a calmness with little pats, and stroked it out with long even motion of her fingers between his and through the passes of his knuckles. Yet her ring's banded gold caught on his bones and rubbed across the skin.

He forgot shame and felt only the energy passing from her to him. She saw his red face, crissed with surface veins like a map with roads, sweat-pored; and then settled with a mist of calm.

ABOUT LEVY

If she can take such trouble with me to lessen fear and strengthen me, then I'm worth noticing; I still have a place where I must stand.

He still lay in his chair, quieted by her steady conduct of his blood. 'Why do you take this trouble with me?' he said. 'I'm a man with a grown-up daughter, yet I'm behaving like a child. Why don't you laugh at me?'

'I've grown out of laughter,' she said. 'I used to laugh always, but it was because I was afraid. I laughed at what I didn't dare to face seriously. I laughed to kill. When my husband drank, I used to make fun of him, the mistakes he used to make in speech, at a false step. I thought I was clever and it would cure him. But he was just wounded that I laughed. He didn't drink any less; a little more, perhaps, but tried to be more and more careful that I shouldn't see he had been drinking. As time went on, I saw quicker and quicker when he had been drinking, and laughed louder and longer, till he grew furious. Then he took up with another woman, who drank too. She didn't laugh at him. They took their drunks seriously. He did this at the golf club. Well, I laughed at *her* too; she certainly was a funny sight. Three parts a man and the fourth an animal. But it wasn't the cure; he went off with her all right.'

'And you've been left?' he said. 'I'm sorry. No, I'm not sorry; I'm rather glad.'

'It's not a nice thing being left. But I'm not sorry now, either.'

ABOUT LEVY

'But that's why you don't laugh?'

'I'll laugh with anyone against the world, but not the other way round.'

'Epigram,' he said, 'or is it epitaph? I can never remember.'

'Never you mind,' she said. 'I should like it to be my epitaph.'

'Talking of laughs,' Mason said, 'he had that sort of laugh. It went through you like a sword. Like a piece of cold steel, it pierced you. You felt you couldn't move, as if you were wounded in some vital part when he laughed.'

'Who?'

'Claude Levy. I never knew where I was with him. It suddenly came like a jet of spurting acid; sort of burnt you to hear him laugh. It made you feel wrong. But I never felt he was laughing at me, or I should have been wild. It was as if he couldn't help it. Yet the curious thing was that he didn't laugh at the things people usually laugh at. He was solemn and silent at those, so that you'd think he had no sense of humour at all. It was at queer things he laughed, suddenly, in great gusts.'

'Yes, he could do that. He was all right. He wasn't married.'

23. The men stood aside in two lines.

'Regular line of honour,' Mrs. Turtle said, and took Miss Ffrancis' arm. 'I feel just as if I was being married again.' She looked at the little woman's blue tailor-made and white shirt and blue tie. 'Only you're not quite a man.'

She unlinked arms as they got into the room.

'Back again; I'm beginning to feel as if this was my own back parlour. Only I'd liven it up with a bit of cretonne, if it really was. We might be the ones in prison by the way they treat us.'

Miss Ffrancis walked away with her hands in her small front pockets.

Mrs. Turtle turned round. 'Hallo, Mr. Mould, it's the last day. Get back to your pots and pans to-morrow.'

'Won't I be glad,' Mould said. He had an Adam's apple which rode between the wings of a butterfly collar, a long throat, which he kept clearing, and shining forehead clustered with sudden curls.

'It's so dull,' she said. 'In *The People* it's all sensations and laughter in court; but not so here. All

ABOUT LEVY

those frosty old jossers in false hair speechifying till me head reels and me throat's as dry as me own bar counter.'

'That's all right, ma. But don't say it too loud or you'll make yourself unpopular round here.'

'Well, I'm fed up messing around here with me old man, what died of a leaking heart, just laid in his grave, and a strange man at the till lunch-times, whom you don't know that you can trust till you find out that you can't.'

'She oughtn't to be 'ere,' Jarrett said. 'Got no sense of the decencies. Who's she to judge a case like this, when she probably can't add up her own petty cash.'

'She's all right,' Freeman said. 'It's men like Chappell there I'm afraid of, with ideas in their heads.'

'I'm a butcher,' Jarrett said. 'They call me "Tiny" at the Foresters'. I stand six foot one in me socks. You wouldn't think I turned the scale at sixteen when I'm stripped; but I do. It's cos I'm big, see. I can carry me weight.'

Freeman lit a cigarette, offered him one.

'I smoke a pipe; always have. Thanks all the same. D'you know Kensal Rise at all?'

'I don't,' Freeman said. 'Why?'

'Stranger to London? Got a chain of slaughterhouses that way, that's all. Yer know, when Alfie—that's my second—came, I was earning forty shillings a week, and ten shillings of that went to paying off the instalment for the house and five shillings for the furniture. Makes you think, doesn't it?'

'It does indeed,' Freeman said.

'And, 'er, Amy—she's my wife—she's got tuber ... consumption, you know; but I'll be an alderman before I'm dead, swear I will; which'll bring roses to 'er cheeks, being called Mrs. Alderman Jarrett.'

'Ah, lunch,' Freeman said.

'Not before I'm ready, neither.'

'Miss Ffrancis, won't you sit here?' Freeman said. He showed her the seat on his left. As foreman, he took the head. 'Mr. Jarrett here and I were discussing whether it would take us long to reach our verdict this afternoon. What do you think?'

Miss Ffrancis looked at him. His hair grew into a silver coxcomb; sharp nose between rat's eyes.

'I don't know,' she said. 'It seems to me to be a very disturbing case, because the man Hall—I suppose I should call him the deceased—appears to have been such an out-and-out rotter.'

'That's a thing which we mustn't take into account at all. It makes no difference.'

'Quite.'

'Our duty is to say whether Levy did it or not.'

'I think that's probably a question which a man can decide very much better than a woman.'

'No. It's not knowledge of men or women, but of human nature. Give you a case of my own. It's a confidence; but we shall never meet again, and confidences are best given to strangers.'

ABOUT LEVY

'I write short stories,' Miss Ffrancis said. 'It might be dangerous!'

'Short stories are almost never published. I'll risk it, if you'll let me!'

'Go on. You've been warned!'

'It's an old story, anyway; but perhaps the more forcible because it happened to me. I'm an engineer, mining chiefly and railroad; have travelled about a bit. I married young, twenty-four, a very beautiful girl; Mexican, with quite a shot of the Aztec blood in her. Met her on the boat from Pernambuco. We were both going up to Vera Cruz. It's quite a way, though it looks close on a map. It looked a fine boat, painted entirely afresh, all white and clean, but swarming in bugs and cockroaches. They crept out as soon as you put the light out; then when you turned up the light, you saw them streaking away, and they were gone. Except, perhaps, a last one which had lost its way, and finally that'd creep out under the door. But that's not here nor there, nor a part of my story. I was young then, and though I fancied myself inoculated, a hard young flint that could strike flame in a lady's heart without catching fire myself, I fell for Bianca; that was her name, you know. I think it's nicer than our Blanche.

'I don't think her eyes were really finer than many other girls' I knew. But she didn't use them so much. She didn't set out to please, but just was pleased. Then her eyes used to shine.

'No, really, all that was wrong with me was I thought

ABOUT LEVY

that if a woman was good-looking she must be good all the way through, and if she was very good-looking, very good. And, besides, her brother had just died, which made me sorry for her; though I don't know whether she cared a damn. No, that's unfair; she did care a damn. But not a very big damn.

'We were married in Mexico City. Her father was a sweaty old rascal. He couldn't smoke a cigar without it coming unrolled, though he looked as if his mother had given him them to keep him quiet instead of a comforter. But Bianca was a joy; though I shuddered when the rascal of a father told me that her mother had been a beauty in her youth, and I saw the dirty old feather bolster *she'd* become. We had two kids, the sort of kids I like, kind of refined *gamin*, like that Spanish man painted, eating sprats. You probably know his name.'

'Murillo?' Miss Ffrancis said.

'Probably that's the name. Then I left her in Toronto. I didn't want to; and she said she wanted to come. But I was going up north into country where she couldn't follow; it was too rough. After all, she was a woman, and there were the kids. So I put her in charge of a man I knew and his wife. She was a nice little woman, though I didn't like him overmuch. You meet some queer people in business. But there it was.

'Well, when I got away in the evenings and work was over, I began to remember things I'd heard about this man. He was a Swede, I think, but born

ABOUT LEVY

in England, and came over to Canada soon after he left school. I remembered I'd heard someone say he wasn't any too nice with women or something vague like that. Then I got letters from her saying how nice he was; how kind he was being to her. And I met a man who knew him quite well, and I drew him on without his knowing, and I found out quite a lot I should have preferred not to. Then I wrote to her, saying she didn't want to cause any scandal, and it might be better not to see so much of him. She wrote to say I was being silly; but she wouldn't, if it would set my mind at rest. After that she didn't mention anything about him. But I found out from a fellow who came up from Toronto that she was always being seen out with him. When I wrote to her about it, she wrote back to say she'd been out with him once or twice because his wife wasn't feeling well and couldn't go; but that was all. I couldn't get any more out of her.

'It got on my nerves, being all that way away, and I couldn't work properly. Couldn't sleep either; than which nothing is worse, I think. Just thinking about it all the time. It got so bad that I finally chucked up the job and went back to Toronto to see what was happening. I didn't let her know I was coming; I wanted to see how things were exactly. I didn't want a fancy husband's home-coming, with "Welcome Home" on the cake. So I just turned up about nine one evening. It was all dark. I went into the kids' room. They were asleep. God, they looked innocent.

ABOUT LEVY

'I sat down by the fire and just waited for the pair of them to come back. Then I thought I was wrong, and rang up my friend's house, and the maid answered the 'phone. I asked if my wife was there. No, she and the master were at the theatre. Did I want to leave a message? I rang off.

'Then I called up the janitor and told him to take my bags round to a hotel. He knew something was wrong; it was hell to see his little leer and tip him.

'It seemed hours waiting. It must have been about an hour and a half. Then I heard them come in. I remember I listened to hear their first words, and I thought "I shall always remember them," the strain was so great. But I don't know for the life of me now what they were. Don't suppose I should recognise her voice even.

'They came in, anyway, as if they were used to it; and I sat, play-acting to myself, looking into the fire. Then she started; I know she did, because I was watching her shadow on the carpet, and she called my name.

'When I looked up, she was running to me and her face seemed really pleased to see me: and it was fresh, and I wanted to kiss her and forget all about everything. I think I would if I had been alone and I hadn't seen the man's face.

'Oh, there was a scene. And he was condescending and slimy, and she couldn't have been more distressed if she had been innocent.'

'And what did you do?' Miss Ffrancis said.

ABOUT LEVY

'I swep' out, and slept by myself in a hotel.'

'Wasn't that rash?'

'Hell,' he said, 'go back? Be each man's fool she met, the *cocu* of the farce. Not I.'

'And what's the point of it all?'

'The point's this. She never admitted. I knew, but she wouldn't give me the satisfaction of it. Her story was that I turned her out; that I was the beast, not she.'

'And what about the other man? Did she marry him?'

'Marry him. He dropped her like a hot brick as soon as I turned her out. Was afraid he might have her on his hands. She got another one though, quick enough. But the point is this, she was spinning yarns like this Levy is, but they didn't take me in. I knew. By the man's face behind her back.'

'That was a long time ago,' Miss Ffrancis said. 'What happened to the kiddies?'

'They were hers,' he said. 'She took 'em. It was quite a time ago. They should be old enough to be gigolos by now.'

24. *When will soup reach me? They talk away from me, bending from Albert Chappell to that spray-hair chap. Oh my, how he talks to that girl, giving so much away, but not for nothing. She thinks, Will he take me out to the Troc for dinner? And what's he doing? He's thinking he'll get away for a business appointment before he goes round to the lady friend's. Cocktails at six, and come as you please. Like that card I saw: La Comtesse de Godknowswhat. That traveller showed me. They say it's the Holy Roman Empire, he says, if you ask. Put an advert in the 'Morning Post': La Comtesse Fanny de Sennegambia has lost her pearls in a taxicab driving from etcetra, £100 reward. No one gets it, see, because she never lost 'em, never had 'em to lose. All she lost in that taxi, 'e says, was 'er virtue, if she had any. But it's an advert, see.*

'E's bringing me soup. I'll say was you born late, son? Before I clear throat, 'e's gone, the best half spilt on cloth. I'd 've said, was you a ten-months baby, George? Why, 'e'd say. I'd 've said, 'cos you're always late. That'd take him down. An' those two'd turn round

ABOUT LEVY

and laugh at 'im and this gap o' cloth be less between us. An' it's cold; least if it was really, it'd be a saving on a day like this; but it's neither. Maggie'd say Laodicean. Bet she would. Like Rover, sit up and beg any number of times. An' the tail wags still across the carpet, thumps on the floor though you'd think 'e was sitting on it. Say neither hot nor cold. Laodicean, dear. Laodicean. What is it? for the Laodiceans are neither hot nor cold. Something like that, only in biblical language; funny the Bible sounds in modern language, vulgar. Wonder what sort of a lunch they give 'im. There's only one of 'im, so 'e doesn't 'ave t' wait so long. Sorry you 'ad t' wait so long, girl said. Where was it? Some station. Looked just like Maggie in that photo, and yet she turned and pressed the till down, gave change, and wiped a glass. I might not 've lived for her. It made me 'eart cry. What did I want, anyway? Fool, it's life. She'd got her own beau, I 'spect, was a nice girl. What did I want sniffin' around?

Can't say the beef's bad; like the brown fat. Funny, s'pose it's roast blood I like best, which sounds bloodthirsty; ha, blood-hungry; ha, a good one; but I can't make it to anyone, because there's no chance. People don't talk about such things. Maggie wouldn't see. She was lovely in that photo. Joy running in her face. Still there in the print. There was the other when she was laughing, which came out all teeth and made 'er wild. But this one looks lovely still. Why don't you frame it, Bert? It's good of Alf, too. I can't frame it, I said. Why not frame it? Go and see, I says. Go and see. She

ABOUT LEVY

turned, and more joy was in her body turning than on all the streets of heaven; and I felt sinking into nothing. That dress stretched tight across shoulders with two ribs of brown from blade to blade as she bent and opened and took it from the drawer. Joy fell from her arms away like a slipping shawl. That braced me. I was limp before, sort of flowing away. She was red, when she turned and said, Why did you cut it? The flames licked round 'is legs, remember, and the print came off the mount, givin' 'im a swollen face most ridic'lous. Cardboard split, buckled, rolling in on 'im and went black over 'is body. I didn't like 'im, that's all. It's not all, didn't like 'im, she says. It was very good of 'im. I thought it was bad of 'im. It was my picture, she says. I took it, I said mild, it was my camera and my film. I developed it and printed it meself. Yes, she said, well? And I cut it up. Aw, you make me sick, she says, and flounces out. Which you do me, I says, after 'er retreatin' back. I felt I'd puke, remember. It's what I loved to tell 'er, all the truth so as she'd think it just a retort as I'm a deep one. Of course, she knew that I meant I wouldn't 'ave it going on the way it was with Alf. I'm sick and tired of this beef, and the potatoes are starchy. She knew. They might give you new ones when you're on a jury. Tell my Member of Parliament. But she only got more open about it. When she said we the first time, I said 'oo? Alf and me, she said. Oh, I said, Alf and you. Sometimes she was kind and coaxed. Funny it's the same woman, and so different since the change came. I knew she wanted something out of me. But she was kind, and I gave it. Sort of made me feel grand, she could wind me round her little finger. But when she'd got another man around, she treated me like dirt. An' it made me feel wild and want to kill the man. Then she gave me a look, an' I knew it was all for me. She didn't care for the man at all. Tinned apricots make me screw me mouth. Funny, skin sticks to yer plate. Ugh, and shape turns me up. Look at that fat chap. He's got on. That riles 'er, that we're still in the same place. See, 'e's having a second. Sort of man who gets on, who can eat shape. Living in the same place and the Walkers moved out to Burgess Hill an' the Clarks to Eastdean. It's not that I can't get on, I said. Well, what is it? she said. An' I wouldn't say. I didn't speak a word. I s'pose it's the same cheese as yesterday. She says, If it's not you can't I s'pose it's you won't. That's my way to say what I mean. I says that's it. I won't. When I married you I married a fool, she says. What did I think? let me see. Yes, only a fool would marry you. It's the same cheese. Knew it would be. Cracked a bit more an' yellower.

'I say,' Chappell said.

The man looked round on his right.

'If they give him this cheese, we won't have to bring in a verdict of guilty.'

'What's that?'

'I said, "Would you like the cheese or a cigarette?"'

'I've got a cigarette, thanks.' The man held one smoking up from his hand. 'Will you have one?'

'I don't smoke,' Chappell said, 'but I've got some in my case if you run short.'

25. Sankey turned up to Commercial Road. The side street was thick with stalls, laden with fruits and vegetables. A ripe young Jewess in a bright cretonne apron was standing by the scales, her hand in a pocket keeping her change.

'How much for the apples, girlie?' he said.

'You can see the price marked,' she said, 'and don't call me girlie.'

'How many pounds have you got in that pile?'

'About twenty,' she said. 'Do you want to buy the stall?'

'It depends,' he said. 'Are you thrown in?'

'Sauce,' she said. 'Get on, what's your business?'

He took the biggest apple from the pile and put a penny down.

'You needn't wrap it up, and keep the change.'

He walked off, digging his teeth into the firm flesh of the apple. When she shouted after him, he looked round and laughed.

The beer in him stirred and warmed him. The bright light, hot stones, and the shouting sieged and

ABOUT LEVY

took his senses. He left this street, turning down Commercial Road. He was strutting on the top of the world. Every woman he passed he could have if he wanted, and he didn't want any of them. Proud with a couple of shillings in his pocket, the rent paid and no work. He was taller than others, and looked down at them as he passed. He looked down on the Jews and their women, rolling like barrels with platted baskets from shop to shop. He threw the spent core into the gutter.

He crossed and turned left-handed up a street. As he went by the children drew aside. His shadow fell on their hands which played. Then right again, down a row of jaundice-brick houses. He went into one of these and up to his room.

The boy came up and knocked; watched his incoming and called him Captain. He thought Sankey was the hell of a person, and Sankey told stories about sailing and foreign towns. Sitting on his bed he taught the boy to tie knots with bits of old blind-cord. The boy bent forward from a broken rush chair, looking at the fingers through shag smoke. Though it hurt his eyes and caught in his throat, he looked down through it at the hands binding cord.

When he half-opened the door, Sankey called, 'Hullo, boy; come in.' He liked having the boy around better than a woman fussing or nagging about money.

The boy came in.

ABOUT LEVY

'Got your job?' he said.

'No,' the boy said. 'There ain't no jobs round here.'

'There are jobs; but the trouble is somebody's always got them.'

'That's it,' the boy said. 'They won't move on. They're afraid of losing 'em and not getting another.'

'Sometimes they move you on, though,' Sankey said. 'Then where are you?'

'In the bleeding soup,' the boy said. He'd been errand boy to a stores when he left school. But he grew older, and there was health insurance to pay. Then he wasn't errand boy any longer; just hung around then, no use to anyone.

'That's this country,' Sankey said. 'There's too much of your bleeding soup in this country. We're up to the neck in it.'

'Up to the eyes and over. But it's the same everywhere. The papers say it's worse in Germany and America.'

'The papers,' the Captain said. 'Who'll give a ha'penny cuss for the papers? Russia's what I say; look at Russia. There's no unemployment in Russia. Why? say the papers, because there's slave labour and they've got to work. Why? say I, because the State's taken the whole shoot over and knows that people have got a right to work, and it gives them work. Russia doesn't keep a man idle, twiddling his thumbs; Russia doesn't give 'em a dole and then curse 'em for taking it. Russia gives men work, men's

ABOUT LEVY

work to do, and they've damn well got to do it. They may talk about conditions in the lumber camps. You've seen what they've said about conditions. I've seen what they've said; and what's more, I've seen the camps themselves. And if that's not enough, I've worked in lumber camps in Canada. Four years of my life I worked there. They just don't know what they're talking about. I say, they don't know what that sort of life is; it's a man's job, not a cissies' party. And all I can say is, if we'd had the things they've got out in Russia, we'd have thought ourselves in heaven or somewhere up-stage like that. They've got proper washing-places and jakes built for them: the river and the woods were good enough for us.'

'Why doesn't it happen here, then?' the boy said.

The Captain laughed. The boy's eyes shining made him laugh.

'Things don't happen because they ought to happen; they happen when enough people want them to and are willing to make them happen. That's what it is, boy. England's what they call a highly developed nation, and you know what that means; every damned foot of it in the towns and every acre in the country is marked and owned by somebody, all of it down to the centre of the earth. England's what they call a nation with a tradition; every one is rooted in tradition. They all say "rooted"; they want to be trees, see. Hearts of oak, they say: I say, blockheads. They want to have a place and belong to the place and the place to belong

ABOUT LEVY

to them. They've spent money on their houses and their mills and their farms. Why should they give 'em up to the State?'

'I see that. I can't see why they should give up money they've spent.'

'You can't see that, boy? No more could I for a time. Till a chap told me a story—Scott, you know 'im, red hair. Scott's got brains.'

'What's the story about?' the boy said.

'It's about a man with twenty sons. Like to hear it?'

'Yes. Is it exciting?'

'It excited me when I heard it. I dunno whether it will you.'

'Go on,' the boy said. The Captain filled his pipe and lit it, drawing the smoke and puffing from the lungs.

'This man died and all twenty came to the funeral; and after it was over and they got back, the eldest read the will, like they do. And the will said that his property was to be divided among the twenty sons. But all he'd got was one grandfather clock.'

'Nothing more?'

'That was all. So they divided the clock into twenty bits, and the oldest took the face because he liked that best, and so each chose in 'is turn, till the youngest had the little hand and the pin that held it to the works. Then they all went away, pleased with themselves because each had got his share. Even the youngest was satisfied, 'cos he kidded himself that the little hand was the nicest thing about the clock, and if he had had to choose first he'd 've chosen the little hand anyway. But when they got home they found that the parts that they had wouldn't go. The oldest stuck the face on the wall, but there weren't no hands to tell the time and no works behind to make the hands which weren't there tell the time, and the youngest found the little hand didn't move of its own, and if it had, there was no face for it to move around. For some time they said: "This is all right; this'll be all right in the end." But it didn't get any better; so they all had a meeting, and the eldest said: "This clock isn't no bloody good any more," and the others said: "My bit won't bloody well go neither." "Well," the eldest said, "you give all the bits to me." "Not blooming likely," they said. So they broke up the meeting. Well, these twenty sons lived in twenty houses next door to one another, like the houses are in this street. And when they got home the brothers thought: "We've only got one clock and that won't go because we've all got bits of it." And nineteen of 'em said: "We're damned if we're going to give him the clock, so that he can have a clock and we have none." And then one of them said: "Supposing we give all our bits to all the rest of us, and then we'll all have a clock and none of us'll have a clock and the rest have none." And that's what they did.'

'But could they get it together again?' the boy said.

ABOUT LEVY

'Well, they could and they couldn't,' the Captain said. 'Some of the bits were so broken or bent that they had to get new ones; and some of the bits just needed mending slightly. But most of 'em with a bit of pulling and shoving went in just as they were made for it.'

'But they couldn't fit them all together by themselves, could they?'

'No, son. That was the point I was coming to. They couldn't do anything without a man what knew all about clocks and how they were put together. And they wanted more than that; they wanted a man, one they could trust. They wanted one to say: "This bit's no good. I know it looks a nice bit and is very old, but it's worn out; it's got to be scrapped."'

'When it was fitted together again, did it go, then?' the boy said.

'Well, it didn't exactly go, but it would've gone if all the rest had happened as I said it did. But what I want to tell you about is the man who could put it together again. You know what race the man was, son?'

The boy said an Englishman.

'Englishman be damned,' the Captain said. 'The man was a Jew. Not a crawling kosher at a stall, not a gayboy neither, nor a flabby, crook-nosed Ikey; that's not what I mean.'

'What d'yer mean then? They're all like Sam Cohen or else Rabinovitch. Or d'yer mean a rabbi?'

ABOUT LEVY

'Not any of 'em. Marx, I mean. I mean Karl Marx. Just a mind—a heart and a mind. No race, no class, no god; just a heart to feel with and a mind to think with. They get off before we do, if you see me. They've got no country from the start, no land they call theirs right to the middle of the earth. We've got to give that up (God spew the man who says we haven't); as the twenty brothers gave up the bits of the clock so that the clock'd work again. They only got to lose their god and they're free.'

The boy stirred on his hams. He wanted knots or stories of the sea. But Sankey went on; and did not look at him.

'D'you see men as I see them? You've got to understand as I understand. But there I end. I'm beat and can go no further. I can't do things no longer; there's a sort of wall against me, and I can't climb it. I've got old, and they laughed at me in "The Grapes" to-day; laughed and wouldn't believe my age. But I didn't see them, didn't see them as men. Saw them as cur-dogs, rather, outcasts—dogs they call pariahs in India, that I've seen hovering round villages and waiting for the shortest sleep to nip in and get the food. Shite hounds they are, not men. Feed on what goes bad in the rich man's larder. But I see real men as quick flame, something that burns and leaps where it wants; how I see them is all bright like polished brass and keen as a razor. I see them put the shite hounds on the lead, setting 'em to hunt real game.'

ABOUT LEVY

The boy stared at him, not understanding. Half of him didn't want to understand. Half of him was a cur cowering back from a torch flashed in his kennel. Half was keen down nosing on the scent, quivering in thoroughbred flanks on a new trail. He thought of the Communists and the red flag song that moved him, and a girl he had seen in a Mayday procession, short-haired, a flame licking her body round, singing that song.

'Why are you saying all this?' he said.

'Perhaps I'm beat,' he said; 'perhaps it's beer on an empty belly. But they laughed at me in "The Grapes," because I talked of Levy, because I stood up for 'im. He's one, I mean. He's a man to make a change come; and if they kill him, there'll be others like him. He's the man who mends a clock, who knows what to throw away and what to keep.'

Bells chimed.

'What's the time?' he said.

The boy went to see.

'Quarter-past four,' he said.

'I must go. It's high tide at half-past five. Shan't be able to get near the bloody gates if I don't go now.'

'May I come?'

'No, don't you come. If I have luck, we'll both have a feed. But you don't come.'

'Can't I come?' the boy said. His voice was pleading, his body ready like a sword half out of sheath.

ABOUT LEVY

'Yes, you can come, if you like. But don't blame me if you get squashed. It's rough there, and men'll shove hard for a job, harder sometimes than they work when they've got it.'

26.   'I have dealt with the accused's own account of what happened during the time between five and six o'clock on the evening of May the eighteenth, and with the arguments for and against establishing jealousy and the desire to prevent the marriage between Miss Mason and the deceased as motives for the accused to commit murder. It is now time to examine the evidence we have of the accuracy of the accused's account.

'We have a check on the accuracy of the accused's account of the interview in the evidence of the finger-print experts. No prints were distinguishable upon the bag; but an examination of the glass showed only the finger-prints of the accused. The inference drawn from this by the prosecution was that only the accused had touched the glass. That he had mixed the poison in the kitchen; thrown the capsule into the lavatory pan, and pulled the plug on it; and then brought the poison to Hall as a pick-me up, and actually held it for him to drink, arguing that Hall himself was incapable of physical effort owing to the alcohol which he had taken. On the other hand, the defence maintains that Hall wiped the stem of the glass with a dish-cloth which was found on the table by the bag, and held it with this cloth while he drank. There were only single impressions of the accused's thumb, index, and second fingers on the stem, though there were numerous other impressions of his fingers higher up the glass. The defence maintains that these single impressions were made on the stem by the accused, when he picked up the glass to smell it.

'Counsel for the prosecution would have you believe that the whole explanation of the defence demands, from those who are to believe it, a degree of disinterestedness in the accused with which it is almost impossible to credit any man; and in the deceased, a quickness of thought and dexterity of execution impossible to a man in his state of intoxication, combined with a cunning selfishness which in its kind is as remarkable as the accused's quality of disinterestedness or interference, whichever you may like to call it. The only explanation which is compatible with what is called human nature is, the prosecution claims, the explanation which they have brought forward. Counsel for the defence, on the other hand, would maintain that, however remarkable the account may be which the accused has rendered of his relationship to the deceased and what happened at the flat, these things are true and happened as the accused says they did.

'Members of the jury, the case is now before you

ABOUT LEVY

to decide on the evidence, without prejudice either against the accused or any other person involved. There is no alternative plea of manslaughter or justifiable homicide; your verdict varies only between innocence and guilt; there is no third course. If you think that the prosecution has made out its case, you must bring in the verdict of guilty. But if reasonable doubt remains in your minds, your verdict will be in favour of the accused.

'Will you please consider your verdict?'

27. Children were sailing boats in the Leg of Mutton pond. They bent down trimming the sails and walked round to the other side. It was past two o'clock now, and the nurses began to wheel perambulators with tasselled awnings.

She telephoned and then went down the hill.

Irène was alone, would see her.

The room into which she was shown was cool and heavily furnished. Everything was so solid that change did not seem to have place here. The atmosphere was as permanent as in a synagogue.

Irène, as she came in, looked fresh; her calm face mounted from a green dress like a tulip among leaves. She kissed Miriam with a quick brush of the lips.

Immediately they were seated, she said, 'I've been expecting you to come sometime.'

Now her fear grew less and she could speak plainly. Before, she had been afraid she might cry. 'I didn't dare go to the trial to-day, and yet I couldn't bear being at home any longer. I went every other day.'

ABOUT LEVY

'Yes, I know you did. I haven't been at all; I didn't feel that he wanted me to be. Thought he might resent it. He likes to fight his battles as much alone as possible. But he needed you.'

'I saw him look at me once or twice, but he didn't show any sign of recognition.'

'Victor said this morning that if there was any need for an appeal he would finance it.'

'I thought he disapproved of Claude.'

'That's when Claude's in a position to be disapproved of. This is different. He's got a very strong sense of family responsibility.'

'You persuaded him.'

'If there'd been any need, I should have done my best,' Irène said, 'but there wasn't.'

'Do you think an appeal will be necessary?'

'I don't know. We've got to be prepared for it, at any rate. These last days have been so queer. Did Claude do it? I feel I know even less about him now than before the trial was begun. You know him better than I do.'

'I'd give anything to speak to him,' Miriam said. 'I don't know now whether he's guilty or not. He seems to have become an entire stranger. But do you think it will make much difference to the verdict whether he did it or not? You remember the Rouse case. They never proved that Rouse was guilty; they hung him because they didn't like his morals, not because he was guilty.'

'Perhaps that was prejudice,' Irène said, 'but I can't see where prejudice can enter in this case.'

'Can't you? I can. Claude's just as much a Jew as we are. It's been brought up against him through his whole life: at that religious school to which he went, where to be as much a Jew as he was conveyed a suspicion of unorthodoxy with it, and at hospital and as a doctor. You remember, he always says that what told much more in his favour than his being a good doctor, was that he was good at rugger. He was tolerated as a scrum half.'

'But being a Jew doesn't make any difference in a court of law.'

'Not ostensibly. But even intelligent people look on Jews as people with entirely different feelings from themselves, whom they can treat according to an entirely different code. They don't have pogroms in this country, but they have economic and social ramps against us. The average Englishman distrusts a Jew in the bottom of his heart. If you'd seen the jury you wouldn't have said they were above the average. Sort of the first twelve men and women you might meet going into Goodge Street Station. I think the fact that Claude's a Jew will influence them quite a lot in their judgment.'

'They're possibly making it now,' Irène said. 'But they won't condemn him just because he's a Jew.'

'It's not the only reason.'

A little figure came from the clock, bursting doors;

ABOUT LEVY

and, raising a trumpet, played a tune. He struck a bell twice. Half-past three. The doors closed back.

Miriam went on speaking. 'Did you ever meet Edith Mason?'

'No.'

'Nor have I. She somehow was never where I was. Claude was always saying that I must meet her: that he thought I would be good for her. But we never met. I never saw her until the trial.'

'What's she like? You can't tell from the papers.'

'It's impossible to tell from the papers; it's impossible for me to say what she's like. She's one of the most beautiful women I've ever met: very black hair and dark eyes; perfect features, except perhaps too full a mouth; big body and well set. You know, there are some people who look so beautiful that it's impossible to believe they can do any wrong or tell a lie.'

'I think I know,' Irène said. 'It's not beauty, but an expression; one sees it mostly in children, usually the naughtiest of them.'

'That's right. But when you meet it in grown-up people, it's overpowering.'

'I don't think I ever have. I seem always to see through them.'

'The jury've met it,' Miriam said. 'So has the judge. While I was in court, I couldn't keep my eyes off her myself. But she's against Claude, I'm sure. Yet she made me believe her evidence while she was giving it.'

ABOUT LEVY

'You think Edith Mason's good looks may count against him?'

'Well, she certainly thinks that Claude murdered Christopher. But there's another difficulty; it makes Claude's account of his proposal to her so much more unlikely. How could he never have thought of marrying her? How could he not want to marry her and yet propose from a sense of duty? And why didn't he introduce us? If he really felt towards Edith Mason as he says he did, why did we never meet?'

'Or if he didn't feel towards her as he said he did, why did he mention her to you at all?'

Miriam looked at the pattern in the carpet, and said, 'Perhaps he forgot; or he said he would and then thought we wouldn't get on with each other; or he just couldn't manage it. Perhaps the reason why he told me was because his mind was so full of her that he had to talk to me about her; but he didn't say that he was in love with her, because he didn't want to hurt me.'

'You can prove anything that way.'

Miriam was rocking her head with her hands. 'Facts,' she said. 'Why can't we have facts quite simply, instead of having to go into reasons and motives.'

'Nothing human is a fact like that,' Irène said, 'except death.'

Why did she say death? Max died in the war, Bruno in an air smash.

Then Irène said, 'Did he tell you of the proposal?'

ABOUT LEVY

'Not before. But I saw him only just before the trial. He told me about it then. That looks as if he suppressed the whole thing to spare my feelings.'

'I always thought he would marry you.'

'No. We both felt it was impossible.' She said this sharply. Then, 'Claude has to be free.'

'I see,' Irène said. 'And do you?'

'Yes, I want to be free, too. Quite free.'

'Does it really satisfy you?'

'Yes,' Miriam said. 'Sometimes I feel I should like to have a home of my own and children. But it would mean leaving Claude. That thought always holds me firm.'

'Him or nothing?' Irène said.

Miriam didn't answer that. 'The difficulty is that my whole idea of him has changed during the trial,' she said. 'I'm sure it'd be all right if I could speak to him. But the description he's given of himself proposing to Edith Mason, and the account of when he was in Hall's flat, though they're just like things he has been doing all along (all part of what he calls his "stunt" in fact); they're just wrong. Explained in a court they rather disgust me. They would have been all right if they had succeeded; but as they failed, it was just interference on his part. If people try to do good and fail, they're busybodies and nothing else. But he's never failed before as long as I've known him. That's over ten years. And what gives me agony is that in this case he may not have failed either.'

ABOUT LEVY

'How do you mean?'

'Well, Christopher was a rotter. Most of us didn't know quite what a rotter he was. I had lunch at "The Spaniards" to-day, and that reminded me. I was there one night with Claude. We used to go there quite often and sit in the garden in the summer. It was convenient, and he liked it. Well, this night Christopher drove up with some of his rowdy friends. They didn't see us, because we were sitting in the garden. He went up to the outside counter and ordered drinks. There was rather a pretty barmaid there at the time, and she used to lean forward very confidentially. Christopher made loud comments on it while she was away. When he had got a beer he beckoned to her, and as she leant forward he poured it down inside her dress. He was turned out, of course.'

'A charming young man!' Irène said.

'Yes. A rotter. Claude was quite right to resent Edith Mason becoming engaged to him. I mean the marriage would obviously have been a hideous failure if it had taken place. He was good for nothing—much better dead. Now what torments me is, that if Claude gave him poison, or forced him to take it, he didn't fail. You see that? What would keep Claude the person I admired, would also mean that he is guilty.'

'If he had done it, do you think he would have put up the defence he has?'

'I don't see any reason why he shouldn't. Having taken the law into his own hands, you wouldn't

ABOUT LEVY

expect him to give himself up and make a clean confession. He believed the good man could do anything; but I don't suppose he believed the law would allow him to do it.'

'Actually I should have expected him to own up if he had done it,' Irène said. 'I've never been able to decide whether he was just a prig or had a great deal of moral courage. I think he might do something which was illegal, but which he considered right: but having done it, he wouldn't deny it; he'd plead extenuating circumstances.'

'Plead manslaughter, do you mean?' Miriam said. 'He couldn't very well have done that.'

'No, I suppose he couldn't, really. But what I was going to say was more complicated than that. Supposing that Claude had been making up a false story, he wouldn't have made one up like this one. It's either too clever or not clever enough for him. It shows his stunt as a failure, himself as a busybody. Claude is too clever to make up a story in which he figures as a fool; and not clever enough to see that that is the best story which he could make up. His pride wouldn't allow him to do it.'

'I see what you mean. He must always be right, and would rather be hanged than plead folly as an excuse.'

'Yes, and more than that. He's not satisfied to be right only. He's got to have other people think that he's right. He can't just go away in a corner and be right all by himself.'

ABOUT LEVY

Time had passed on without their noticing. The sun swung round and slanted on to the writing-desk. The papers there began to buckle. The heat of day found even this cool room out. When she had come in, it was remote from the world of sailing boats and coursing and Claude. But now the cries of children, returning to tea, pierced shrilly in and Claude, his white revolutionary face, his unquiet spirit ranged it, energising her to no purpose.

'We'll have tea now,' Irène said.

'Thanks,' Miriam said, 'I must go.'

28.   'LIFE's only what it is,' Mason said, 'and you've got to take it how it is; because if you try and make it something else, you'll lose what you have and won't get what you want to have.'

'There's not time to remake things: we don't live long enough. That's true. If we all do our little bit in our own little way, that's all that's asked of us.'

'These fellows that want everything changed are all very well.'

'You won't change human nature, Charles.'

'No, you can't. And if you try, you just make yourself miserable; and other people miserable as well.'

'I suppose you're thinking of your friend Levy.'

'Not exactly my friend; say I knew him, and you'll be nearer the mark. Yes, I was thinking of him when I spoke just now. He was a world shaker for you. There wasn't anything he didn't want changed in some way. It was all reform with him. Medical reform, legal reform, divorce-law reform, asylum reform. There wasn't a damn thing but he found something wrong with it that ought to be put right.'

'Crank?'

'That's what I called him. "What does it matter?" I used to say. "Why do you waste your breath? Why don't you wait till you want to be divorced before you get excited about it?"'

'What did he say to that?'

'He said that was the one time you couldn't agitate about it.'

'I don't see that. That was just being clever.'

'I don't know. He said things that turned common sense tail upwards. I never knew whether he did it just to be clever in talk or because he really believed it. But I think I understand what he meant this time. If you're going to interfere you must make sure that there's nothing to gain for yourself by doing it.'

'That sounds a sort of losing game, like losing draughts. Have you played them? It's so queer, because when you're a bad player like me you feel you can't help losing, but I get all mine crowned before I've thought of starting.'

'Rum,' Mason said. 'Yes, Levy's game's rather like that. But it just won't work. I'm a business man, and I look at things from a business angle. It's natural a man should. I said to him, "Imagine a business run on those lines. What it boils down to is this: you have an article I want. I offer you money for it. We both gain by the transaction. You get your profit and I the goods. But if anyone adopted your principle, he'd say, 'if I gain anything from this transaction I cease to be a disinterested party, so I will give you the article.' You can't go on doing that." '

'But it's not the same case,' she said. 'Getting a law passed in his way is for the general good, a business transaction is merely for the good of private people. Aren't I right?'

'Of the two parties. Yes, I suppose you're right. It is different. But that was the sort of argument we had. And we never agreed. I said people worked because they got money for it, and he said they ought to get money because they worked; they should be given enough to live on and then do the work. I said, "Do it for the love of the thing?" "No," he said, "because it's there to be done." But I expect this bores you.'

'No, Charles, really.'

'Let's have tea; I'll get them to bring it out here.'

'That would be lovely. Do you think they will?'

'Of course they will, if I tell them to.'

He got up with some difficulty from his chair and rolled towards the house. His coat was caught above his buttocks like a shawl across the forehead just above the eyes. It looked like a great jowled smiling face, and disappeared through the doorway.

Mrs. Failey opened her bag and drew her compact from its pocket. She peered into the mirror. The skin grown coarse, sweat had drawn lines upon the powder; the skin beneath the throat was scarlet with sunburn and the pores distended.

She said, 'Poor face,' and began to hide it under dabs of powder.

Then she took the stick and lined the lips even to the edges. It made her feel new.

Pathetic old porpoise; yet no one in the place more possible. I grow old. What part of me is attracted to vulgar, middle-aged men? Wouldn't like him anywhere but here. Am a bitch. Yet he seems real enough here, except in the baths. And I understand him. Just wants his hand stroked.

He came back smiling.

'Is it all right?'

'They'll bring it out here directly.'

'The way you manage them is wonderful,' she said. 'You're so resolute. They'd never have brought it out here for me.'

'I can get my way in most places.'

'Except in the home?'

'There, too, if I wanted. I mean, I'm not a person who's easily diddled. People can't take me in any more than they can stand out against me when I want a thing done. In the City they say of me, "Mason can get things done when no one else can, through sheer persistence." '

She was suddenly terribly bored. His conversation was as dull as his showing her snapshots of himself. 'This is me at Trouville.' 'Here I am riding a mule up the Siebengebirge.' 'This is my office, the desk at which I sit.' 'I have an office chair which swivels round' (*so that he can see things from a business angle?*)

She wiped a yawn away with her handkerchief. A maid was coming with a tray across the grass. The sun struck down her face and dress.

'Here's tea.'

'Good.' He rubbed his hands. 'Have you tasted their blackberry jelly?'

The maid came stepping with the pride of youth, conscious of her ripe breasts, whose shade the sun threw down her dress. She put the tray down on the table, condescending. The smile was a gift from abundance.

Mrs. Failey thought, 'Five years; I give her five years before the teeth go. Two more for the arches to fall. Children will do the rest.'

But Mason watched the flexile bending of her hips and the cream lace collar bowered about the neck. He did not look at the red hands, spoiled with soda.

'Do you think Levy was in love with your daughter, Charles?'

'Eh?' he was looking after the girl. 'I really can't say. He never seemed to me to have ordinary feelings; no eye for a pretty face or figure. He certainly never spoke about that sort of thing. He often said things before ladies that made me blush; but he had no feeling for a smoke-room story.'

ABOUT LEVY

'I'm interested in this losing game idea of his.'

'He was always talking about it. He had a great phrase for it, let me see ... oh yes, 'the quintessence of Christianity.' He said the quintessence of Christianity is to believe in everybody so completely that they can't betray you. The only man who can't be attacked is the man who offers no resistance. And more of the same sort. It sounded all nonsense to me. It just doesn't work.'

'Judas Iscariot proved it didn't work.'

'Yes,' he said. 'Will you have a cigarette?'

She took one. He bent over to light it for her, holding the match shielded in his great hand. Then he lit his own and poked the match stub into the dry earth. They both lay back in their chairs. The shadow of the tree was edging off them. His mind was back in its prospected land; where sign-posts pointed to profit or loss, a country of commercial travellers. But her mindscape was wisped with scarves of mist through which the things that appeared to her were not definite or whole. Their parts were strange, and of a texture that she did not know. Nothing was clear except their novelty, exciting novelty. But she did not even know whether she wanted this excitement. She said, 'But they could say that Judas' suicide, or the Resurrection and Christianity proved it did.'

A robin perched on the table and pecked at the bread and butter. Its legs were always ready to spring, its wings to open for flight. But it remained, pecking in quick timid jerks and watching with unflinching eye.

'Pretty,' Mason said.

It flew away on to the branch of a tree; where it rested, looking down at him.

29. Ruth stood with her right hand on the knob. Then she turned it and the key with her left and pulled the door open.

The nurse was waiting outside, and started at the sudden opening.

'You wanted me?'

John's voice rose in a cry, fell and rose.

'Yes, medem, there are a few things wanted for the children.' Then she turned to the child: 'Raight, darling, Nannie won't be a moment.'

'What are they?'

The nurse handed her a list. 'Perhaps you would prefer me to get them for you.'

Ruth took the list and said, 'No, I'll get them, thank you.'

'We usually have the large packets of Thermogene,' the nurse said.

'I know that. Is that all?'

The girl's face shone, knobbed with two moles. John was at the door again, waiting to run to her. 'Don't let him trouble you to-day, medem,' the girl said, 'not to-day.'

ABOUT LEVY

Ruth held her arms down ready to take him, and as he came running closer she bent till she was sitting on her heels.

The girl, stooping, said, 'I know what you're suffering.' Eagerly, 'I've been through it too.'

John ran into her bosom and, with arms round her neck, tried to climb his knees on to her lap. He put up his mouth and kissed her full on the lips.

'It was bankruptcy in our case. Ai shouldn't be here if it wasn't for that.'

Ruth said, 'There, there,' to the boy.

The girl pulled down his jersey, saying, 'What a mess you're in; you've been getting into some mischief, I can see.'

'I'll see to it, nurse,' Ruth said. 'Will you go and look after Hugh?'

The nurse went along the passage, stopped at the nursery door, turned and then went in.

Ruth bent over John and said, 'Who do you love best in all the world?'

30. EDITH went to her room, which seemed strange to her. She looked at the furniture as if she saw it first again after long absence. Was it really like this? Had this bed always a beaded pattern at the head? Had the curtains a waving pattern of thread beneath the colour? Was the room so small?

She lay down on the bed; the full light fell on her face. She was stretched, looking upwards at the sun. Then she got up and pulled the curtains and locked the door. The light was diffused by the stuff of the curtains, but here and there it seeped through a point and burst into a star. She turned her head to the pillow and pressed her face into it. The linen drew in and fitted across her mouth when she breathed.

The tap dripped into the basin.

When he was in the box he was away from me. Nothing that I said could wound him. He would not let me pity him. When he was in the box he spoke of me as if I was a stranger or his patient.

ABOUT LEVY

A door rap. The knob tried. Another rap. She pressed her head deeper in towards the pillow.

'Edith, Edith.'

She would not speak.

'I've brought you some coffee.'

'I don't want any coffee. Take it away, please, and leave me alone.'

She listened. A clink of china.

'I've left it outside for you on the mat.'

She did not answer.

'Do you hear? I've left it outside on the mat, dear; in case you change your mind.'

She beat her hands on the bed.

'And if there is anything you want, you've only got to ring and I'll be up in an instant.'

The footsteps went away. Everything was still. The tap dripped into the basin.

Suddenly she burst out crying, and it made herself sad to listen.

Then after a time footsteps came softly and stopped by the door. She held in her breath so that she could not sob. A car passed in the street. The noise was like a hand passed over the room. Was there someone standing outside? A shoe creaked.

The footsteps went away. Her eyes had cleared, and she saw, on the pillow, marks of rouge from her lips. She drew her hand across her mouth. It was smeared red.

She got up, went to the basin and turned the cold

ABOUT LEVY

tap; then took a flannel and, dipping in the water, dabbed her face with it and drew it hard over the lips, rubbing until they were clean pink. They were clean pink and except the flesh beneath the eyes, which was sullen with weeping, her face was smooth over bone. The sight made her feel good.

She stood looking at herself for a time and took courage. Then she turned away and pulled back the curtains and drew a chair to where she could see the street.

She said aloud, 'I must think.' She watched two errand boys cycling in wobbling courses down the street. 'I must think.'

She lowered her head on to the prop of her arm, and looked at the cross of her legs beneath her dress. *I ought not to have said Chris never threatened he would do himself in. Remember his tall body bowed at that moment, the mouth pulled down at the edges, so much a dog before me. But then he said, will you swear that you will never tell anyone of this; that it will be a secret between us? and I said, yes. At that moment he was utterly at my mercy, would have done anything that I wished; I had only to say the word—he would have knelt down and kissed my feet. He can never say I didn't keep my promise. If I had told, they would have said that he had committed suicide. That would have been the end. The whole truth and nothing but the truth, so help me, God. If they hang you, Claude, I shall always think it was I who was responsible.*

Two dogs met and snarled—a collie and a chow.

ABOUT LEVY

The collie snapped; the chow was on his neck. Two women came up. Each stood waiting for the other to do something. The dogs chased each other's tails. Was it fun? Quickly the collie turned, seized the other's ear. The chow shook him off and jumped and they rolled over and over, a mass of fur snarling. The porter came from the flats opposite—the collie was his —and threw a pail of water over them, and the ball unrolled into two dogs. He tried to kick the chow; but it avoided his foot and walked off, always turning head to see it was not being attacked from the rear. The collie followed the porter in at heel.

I must go and explain. I can say that I had forgotten; that it has suddenly come back into mind. They will never know, if I don't tell them. But I shall always know. It is the only thing I can possibly do. I must go and tell them. Then if Claude is condemned I'll not hold myself responsible.

She sat in her chair, watching the street where the dogs had fought and so suddenly parted. She laid her hand along her face as gently as a lover's and felt its smoothness.

Her blood pulsed faster in her body. 'I won't say that I had forgotten and it has suddenly come back into my mind,' she said. 'I'll say that I intentionally suppressed it. That's what I shall say; because he might be acquitted.'

31. The paper was folded on the table. A head-line in thick type, LEVY MURDER TRIAL; a photograph of a bending blur between two policemen, 'The accused leaving court after yesterday's session.'

It fell into the paper-basket with a plop. Ruth pushed the basket to the side of the desk.

On the first day he was as calm as calm. He always tucked back the hair that fell forward on to his forehead. Then for a little while his forehead was high. Then he bent forward like the judge, listening, and it slipped down again. The court was as quiet and cool as a grave. Edith Mason looked very becoming in black. Those half veils suit her. Not my type, though David thinks they are. He always wants me to have the best of everything.

She walked down the stairs, it not being worth while really to use the lift, because you've got to wait for it to come up, and it's evens whether anyone's using it. Anyway, the exercise was good.

There was kidneys and a small packet of Atora. I never knew him. It seems terrible for such a thing to happen, really it does. Packet of soapflakes, dozen of matches. The tea-towels can wait. Get them at the sales. It might be anybody else's brother. I should be just as sorry. I know there's something else.

Mrs. Derrick and Miss Lowe have just come out of the café. They are stopping; will they come? They come this way. I know there's something else.

'Good-morning.'

'Fancy meeting you, Mrs. Abrahams.'

'You can see where I'm bound for, Mrs. Derrick.'

Miss Lowe said, 'Mrs. Derrick and I have been having such a set-to. Haven't we, Mrs. Derrick?'

The other woman didn't answer. *She still uses that awful green powder.*

'Perhaps you can help?'

'I'm sure I can't,' Ruth said. 'What is it?'

'It's about your poor brother. Is he guilty? What do you think? I'm sure he can't be guilty; he's so *spirituel*, as the French say.'

'I'm afraid I can't help you,' Ruth said. 'You'll know in a few hours, if you buy a paper.'

'I'm very grieved, Ruth, for your sake,' Mrs. Derrick said.

'There's no need to be sorry for me.'

'But it's such a shock. Will you come round to tea next Wednesday, and we'll have a real chat?'

'Not next Wednesday, but sometime. I must hurry or I'll never get home again.'

They said good-bye.

Cats. There's something else. She'll know in a few

hours' time. Ronuk, yes. To-day is bright sun, which I had forgotten. Bowl on table. Ronuk is all. And I shall know, too, in a few hours. Mother looks down from heaven. Thank God she's dead. Does it move her, or is she just as she died?

This is Castle's; cool and clean with sawdust on the floor. Am I upset by this at all? What a smell of cheese! Or am I cast so down that I cannot feel?

32.   FREEMAN laid his watch before him on the table and leant forward in his chair.

Someone said, "Sh.'

They all looked his way.

He said: 'Ladies and gentlemen, during this trial and the summing up I've made various notes, and have drawn up the issues to be decided in the form of questions. I don't know what form of procedure is usual in cases of this sort, but in the only other jury on which I've served before, the foreman put the questions before the jury; these were voted upon; then, if there was any disagreement, the minority of the dissentients gave their reasons and there was a general discussion. Does that appeal to you?'

Two people said, 'Yes.' Then someone said, 'Aye.' Then all the rest said, 'Aye.'

'Well, we're all busy people here, and we've all got jobs waiting for us to do. We've already spent a considerable time on this case; so, without wasting any more, I'll propose my first question without further ado.

ABOUT LEVY

'(1) Did the deceased wipe the stem of the glass
in the kitchen, as he is said to have done; or
'(2) was the accused himself responsible?'

'What's he saying?' Mrs. Turtle said. 'I can't hear a word.'

'Speak up, please, Mr. Foreman,' Mould said. 'We can't hear down this end.'

'I'll repeat it,' Freeman said louder.

'(1) Did the deceased wipe the stem of the glass,
as he is said to have done, or
'(2) was the accused himself responsible?'

'What have we got to do?' Mrs. Turtle whispered.

'Hold your hand up,' Mould said.

She, Chappell, and Mould held up their hands.

'Please understand the form of the question. If you think the deceased wiped the glass himself, hold up your hands.'

Mrs. Turtle lowered her arm. 'I don't know,' she said. 'Why did you tell me to hold up me hand?' Mould didn't look at her. 'Making a fool of me.'

The rest looked at him and Chappell.

'Mr. Chappell,' Freeman said, 'will you state your reasons first.'

Chappell turned red, and all his time of speaking played with a pencil, dropping it between finger and thumb, drawing it through to the other end with his other hand and letting it drop again. 'I should like first to protest against the way you are putting these questions, Mr. Foreman. It seems to me quite unfair to put them that way round.'

'Hear, hear,' Mould said.

Chappell turned round to him; then he went on, 'Though I have no objection to your dealing with this case in the form of questions, I feel you are putting them in the wrong way. I mean, I believe there are certain of us who are very uncertain about this case, and yet we are not prepared to give reasons before the others.'

'Hear, hear,' Mould said.

'Order there, please.'

'But, do you see what I'm driving at? If these people's opinion is going to have any weight (and I think the fact that they are uncertain is of some importance) you ought to put the questions in favour of the accused.'

Mould said, 'Yes, only the people who were prepared to talk, put up their hands then. You ought to put the question round the other way. And, what's more, those people who think him guilty ought to give their reasons first.'

'I appreciate your point, Mr. Chappell. And I will put the question the other way: Will those who think that the accused and not the deceased wiped the glass, put up their hands?'

Six people put up their hands. A seventh did slowly. Freeman looked round the room. No more held up hands.

'Thank you,' Freeman said. 'I think we shall have

ABOUT LEVY

to deal with another question first. Because that is where the basis of disagreement is likely to be. That question is, Can the accused's evidence be accepted? I think that is the way you want the question put, isn't it?'

'No,' Mould said. 'Is the accused's evidence to be disbelieved or doubted, or whatever the word is?'

'In that form, then. Is the accused's evidence to be doubted? Those who think "yes," hold up their hands.'

The same seven held hands up.

'Would one of those seven people like to explain why he doesn't think it is to be believed?'

There was a silence.

'The way I look at it is this,' Miss Ffrancis said, 'Anybody who is accused of murder isn't very likely to admit it. He wants to live. Very few people admit to having committed murder, and those who do so either do it under the impulse of conscience or because they think they will get off more lightly by pleading guilty to manslaughter or something. I don't think the accused has got that sort of conscience; he would probably say to himself, if he was guilty, "Well, I'm much more use than this man was; but the law won't see that. Anyway, that's not the question now: the question is, 'Am I to go on living or not?'" And his answer to that would be, "Yes, I like living; and, besides, I am of some use to the community. So I'll go on living if I can." I think we can be quite certain that if he was guilty, he is the sort of man who would use all his wits to get off.'

ABOUT LEVY

'But you're assuming all the time, lady, that he is guilty,' Mould said. 'Now, what if he's not?'

'I was just coming to that. Supposing that he's not guilty, then his story must be possible. It must have been able to take place.'

'It could have taken place,' Chappell said.

'You think it could; that it's physically possible?'

'I do,' Chappell said.

'I don't know whether you've ever been drunk, Mr. Chappell,' Miss Ffrancis said. They tittered.

'No, madam.'

'To my shame, Mr. Chappell, I have. It was a long while ago. But during my unfortunate lapse from sobriety I found sustained thought difficult and the co-ordination of thought and action impossible.'

'That was because you wasn't used to it, lady,' Mould said. 'It's surprising the things a man can do when he's drunk.'

'That's true,' Mrs. Turtle said. 'There was a man in my house dead drunk, blind to the world, as you might say, and we sent round for his missis. And she came round, and all she said to 'im was, "Get up, you dirty sot, you," and 'e got straight up and walked out. It's true that as soon as he got outside he fell down on the pavement and cut his eye open and had to be taken 'ome in a cab. But he did that thing.'

'That is very interesting, Mrs. Turtle,' Freeman said, 'but . . .'

'It's true,' she said.

ABOUT LEVY

'I have no doubt it's true, but I'm afraid what little light it throws on the case is in favour of what Miss Ffrancis has said. The fact that the man fell unconscious on the pavement shows that sustained action is not a thing found in an advanced stage of drunkenness. Now, what the accused wishes you to believe is that two things were possible: one, that Hall was capable of a very complicated action, and, secondly, that he was so drunk that Levy could think that he was suffering from the effects of alcohol when he came reeling into the room, actually contorted with the pain of the prussic acid. Think of the whole act. Suicide never before mentioned by Hall (who seems to have been the sort of person who'd talk about it for years before he put it into practice): the use of the doctor's prussic acid; the idea of taking a glass to fetch the doctor some water:— the doctor might never have coughed—what would he have done then?—his being capable of shutting the door and removing the bag silently, and taking the glass and the bag into the kitchen: his conceiving the idea of making Levy appear as the murderer: his wiping only the stem of the glass, and drinking the poison with the rag round the stem, so that his prints shouldn't be seen: his going and pulling the lavatory plug. And then his return, staggering under the poison; yet already so far gone in whisky that the doctor thought he was just drunk. The whole thing to me is inconceivable.'

ABOUT LEVY

He paused.

'Then, another thing. The accused said that he pulled the lavatory plug, having dropped the case of the capsule into the pan. Now what could be the point of Hall's doing that? It was what he, the accused, did, in order to hide his tracks. In my opinion, it's a thing that he might have thought of, but not the deceased.'

'I say the point of Hall's doing that was to make it look as if Levy had murdered him,' Chappell said. 'You say Levy would have done it. I say, that's why Hall did it.'

'But I mean it's scarcely a thing a sober man would think of,' Freeman said.

'A drunk man might, though,' Mould said. 'It sometimes makes you think like mad.'

'Makes you worry. Think perhaps about things that are deep down in your mind; of things that have happened before. But you don't think out new things.'

'Speak for yourself,' Mould said.

'No, but it's absurd.'

'The lady said it was physically impossible,' Chappell said—'and so did you, Mr. Foreman—to do those things when drunk. You've apparently got the advantage of me in experience. But when you say "impossible" each time, don't you really mean "improbable"? It seems to me we can't say these things are impossible.'

'No; not even if we couldn't do them ourselves,' Mould said.

33. 'I EXPECT it's all over now,' Mrs. Failey said. 'Yet we shan't know till the News Bulletin.'

'It's all relative, isn't it?' Mason said. 'All we care is whether we know or not. From the logical point of view, after the decision's made, we should stop worrying; because we can't do any good. But we go on worrying till we hear.'

'From the logical point of view we shouldn't worry at all, because we can't do any good by it.'

'Yes, we mustn't worry. But I've been troubled lately. I can't sleep. As soon as I close my eyes I begin to see things.'

'What sort of things?'

'I see all things before a dark screen. Sometimes it's shapes which seem to be lit from behind, there's only a rim of light round their shapes and their body is all dark. These move—ribbed fans they are sometimes, and sometimes arrowheads across the screen.'

'How do you mean they move?'

'They pass slowly across my eyes, and sometimes

ABOUT LEVY

stop and move back. And sometimes the darkness clears in the centre and I see through it, as though I was looking down, some object, an inkpot I remember, and a shell; one of those big Pacific things. These are all in colours.'

'Queer! And you see things you've never seen before?'

'Never before these things, but things like them. For instance, last night I saw my daughter naked as she was born, if you'll excuse me, lying flat, still upon a floor.'

'Yes?'

'Yes; and a bar of light fell on the floor and across her body sideways, and there was a pot of cactus—one of those spiky ones, you know—between her and the light, which threw a long shade between her breasts. It made me afraid.'

'Perhaps it was a dream.'

'It was no dream; I tell you, I was awake all the time. I can't sleep for the things I see.'

'What happened next?'

'That's what I said. "What's going to happen next?" as I watched her lying there. And I looked hard at the face to see if it was Edith certainly, and she was gone and it was all darkness. It always happens when I bend my whole attention that the sight goes.'

'It makes you think.'

'It certainly makes you think. I'm not a book-learned man, in education. But it makes me think

ABOUT LEVY

what is going on behind me, when these things come out as soon as my mind's half asleep.'

'It's like mice, which come out when no one's around, and scuttle back at the first footstep,' Mrs. Failey said.

'Rats in the attic. Perhaps that's it.'

They laughed.

'I didn't mean that, Charles,' she said. 'Really I didn't.'

'I don't mind,' he said, 'but listen to what I was going to say. I'm normal. As average a man as you'd find in a day. Well, if I see these things, if there are these mice in my house, it must be the same with every one. They can say what they like, but they must be there.'

'What do you mean?'

'This is what I mean; that Claude Levy may pretend and pretend that he does what he does, because it's his duty, but how does he know? It's just a pose to be disinterested. So that he can blame me and I can't blame him. That's all it is.'

'But does he blame you?'

'Of course he doesn't. But when I said "Me," I meant anyone. Anyone you please. Who's he to say who's right and who's wrong? When there are rats in his attic too.'

She took a cigarette from her case and fitted it to a holder.

He leant over and lit it, and still leaning as for a secret said, 'That's why, when you said did I think

ABOUT LEVY

Claude was in love with Edith, I wouldn't say. If I believed what my eyes saw only, I should say, "No, emphatically no." He has no sex, could never love anyone except himself. But he had her, you see; she went to him rather than to her mother or me. In a way, even if he wanted to attract her physically, his way was the right way of going about it. And then there are these mice that don't come out when the mind is around. His mind was everywhere when I saw him; there was no place for the mice to be, unseen. But they must have been there, breeding in the dark, and perhaps they came out into the open when they were strong enough.'

'When there were so many of them that they couldn't stop behind the wainscot any longer?'

'That's the idea.'

The sun was covered by a bank of rising cloud. A breeze blew cold across the grass.

Then Mason said, 'Getting quite chilly.'

'We'd better go in,' she said.

'I've been talking a lot. It must have made you tired.'

'Oh, no.'

They got up.

He took her bag and said, 'I don't know about you. But it's made me thirsty anyway.'

34.   'You're too young for this job,' Captain said. 'You just stand around while I see what can be done.'

The boy walked at his side without speaking.

'Why, I don't know that I shall get anything myself,' Captain said. 'It's a gamble, see. Maybe I do, maybe I don't.'

'They're all going this way,' the boy said.

'Trying yer luck, mate?' a man said, coming up with them.

'Bet yer life,' Captain said. 'All vultures after the same bloody corpse.'

'That's it. And the youngster, is he coming too?'

'Him? No, he's going to hang around.'

'Mascot?'

'That's the idea. When does she come alongside?'

'Half an hour,' the man said. 'Shouldn't be late.'

They turned down to the yard. The alley was filled with standing men. They were still coming up.

'God blimey,' the man said.

They joined the edge. A few feet away men were

ABOUT LEVY

stacked together like cattle in a pen, and raised their heads to the air. Cries came from near the gates. The shaft of men was slowly edging nearer the gate, and some were being crushed against the wall and gates. The cries rose: 'Get back.' 'Get back there, blast you.' Each man looked round at his neighbour, waiting for him to give ground so that he might get in front.

A few yards from them a tall man raised his elbow and rammed it back into a smaller man's face. 'You get back where you bloody well was.'

'Wasn't moving,' the small man said. 'They're pushing me from behind.'

'You clear away from here, boy,' Captain said.

'I'll stay with you,' the boy said.

'You'll bloody well clear out when I tell you,' the Captain said.

The boy went. He had to push a way through the layers of men who had come after them.

'Would come,' Captain said.

''E's gone now,' the man said. 'Not before it was time neither.'

'What's the time, anyway?'

'Twenty past.' The man nodded to the warehouse clock.

'Quarter of an hour more,' Captain said.

The alley was narrower where it joined the road than at the gates; so that there was a tendency to wedge and bottle the men tighter the more they pressed in.

ABOUT LEVY

The boy went round to the side of the alley away from the Captain and stood a moment. Then he went up to the edge of the press. The men were turned away from him. 'Can I come through?' he said.

'What d'yer want?'

'Got to see dad; mother's taken bad.'

'Where is 'e?'

'In the yard.'

'You'll never get through.'

'I've got to get through.'

'Have a try,' they said; 'make way there.'

The first line let him through and said, 'Make way.' Gradually he worked up, between the men. Now held up and squashed—now his way cleared. But when he was still some fifteen yards from the door a whistle blew, and he saw the moving masts beneath the roof of the shed. All the men murmured; then they were quiet, and the whole crowd moved a yard towards the gates. His face was thrust between the shoulder-blades of the man in front of him. He levered room to breathe, with his fists in the back of the man in front. But the tension on his muscles was so great that his arms trembled. The man in front, feeling the pressure of his fists, half turned and said, 'What the hell you doing?' He couldn't answer as his fists lost hold and his face was jerked forward. The knob of the man's shoulder caught him in the eye.

Then they cried, 'They're open.' And the fighting began. Each tried to pull back the next.

ABOUT LEVY

'Seventy wanted.'

'How many?'

'Seventy.'

There were three hundred men driving their weight down the bottle neck. The boy was in midstream, and caught along with the struggling centre. There was a lag at each side. Men were pinned against the sides, and used all their strength to avoid being squashed; or they were caught against the drain pipes and could not push their way round.

By the gates the alley turned up right, and there was a stagnant corner on the left where men eddied but could not get into the solid stream that pushed slowly through the gate. If you got too far on the right, the pressure splayed you out into the side alley as soon as you got past the building. A man tried to get back, running like mad into the crowd. He failed first time, and the next a man caught him on the jaw with his fist. Someone pulled him away to the wall.

The boy was carried right to the narrow entrance by the gates. Then he felt a pressure to edge him to the right, turning him aside.

He didn't know how many men they'd got, but was afraid each would be the last. Though he was not so strong as they, he was thinner and took up less room. He banged in left, and the stream carried him right up to the gate. The foreman gave him a card. Then he went on in.

He thought of the Captain, and turned round to

ABOUT LEVY

look through the gate. He saw him fighting with another man near the gate to get in, and shouted, 'Come on, Cap'n.'

Captain saw him. The boy could see the surprise cross his face.

They put up a board, 'No men needed.' The crowd was pushed back. Someone said, 'Get back there,' and slammed the door.

Then the boy turned again and followed the others to the dock sheds.

35. THE fields were quiet and rich. The cows advanced across the grass in a rough diamond, and, as they swung their tails, steadily cropped the grass. That was the only noise. They fed as a herd, ranging the field. But when they chewed the cud, they split into groups. *Strumer told us to look at cows; then Claude and I watched them, their slapping udders and sacklikeness through which the bones stuck when they were lying down, in which the bones moved when they moved, as if the bones were alive but the flesh on them was dragging dead. How the cow's head full-face is stupid, but in profile noble. Remember Claude said, Europa must have seen Jove in profile, or she'd never have got on his back.*

He had been going on to the pool by which they had found the lark's nest in the young hay; but he turned back. The fact that everything was so much the same here, but every person so different, made him sad. He didn't want to see any more. It was better to be back with the people.

The match was working itself out. Peacock had

got 50. Lomas was out for 2, which brought his average down to 29.5. Lucky boys ate strawberries from baskets their mothers had brought them. Lonely boys took their mothers to see the scout ground, where they were weaving mats from hay or plaiting baskets out of reeds.

Langtry was in great form: his voice, raucous with phlegm, whisky, and tobacco, bellowed 'No ball,' 'No run,' or 'Move that damned screen,' with equally unctuous anger.

The women said to every one they met, 'What a wonderful day for Commemoration Day. I told the headmaster he was lucky to have such fine weather, because it *is* a dreary function when it's wet.' Where men met there were fragments of conversation: 'The trial on Commemoration Day, a queer coincidence.' 'Bugler, the swindler, was an old Rockleyan too.' 'Have you heard what Edith's ma's on?' 'I was stopping at a hotel where there were two chorus girls living on the top floor, who said . . .' 'Which only shows, doesn't it?' 'If it's true.' 'Oh, it's true all right.'

Strumer came up and said, 'Come home and have tea. My wife's away, but I can make it easily enough. I'm tired of this damned match and these bloody parents.'

Common followed him to his car.

'Seen Bubb?'

'Only for a moment,' Common said.

'You were lucky. He did a splendid thing, they say,

in going to India. The only thing I deplore is that he troubled to come back.'

'He's recovering from dysentery.'

'He's sniffing round here for a job again, if you ask me. Still, the man we've got now is a fool; we couldn't go any worse, even with old Bubb. The present man's only interested in wireless and the mass; in that order.'

'I'm surprised to see you still here,' Common said.

'So am I. I should have thought they would have sacked me before now.'

'I don't think that: you've become a "character," so that nothing you do or say matters. But I expected you would have left.'

Strumer took the corner too fast. If anything had been coming they couldn't have avoided a head-on collision.

'I know this road rather well by now,' he said.

Then he said, 'I lost the boat. I thought it would call for me, but it doesn't come up backwaters like this. I'm a sort of John Gabriel Borkman who never even had the opportunity for failure. . . . But tell me about Claude Levy. Have you seen him?'

'I told you I'm only just back from abroad.'

'Of course, I'd forgotten that. Claude was able. He could have got a schol. easily if he'd wanted to. Have you read the case?'

'No, not all of it.'

'It was very interesting on the evidence they've got. He's succeeded in countering all their evidence

ABOUT LEVY

with alternative explanations. But you never know what's going to happen in a murder trial. He's been so damned proud. Hasn't crept to them at all.'

They stopped before the cottage, got out, and went in.

'Excuse the mess,' Strumer said, 'I've been pigging it while I've been alone.'

Strumer cleared out breakfast. The furniture and its arrangement was just as when Common had been there while he was at school; but shabbier.

When he came back Common said to him, 'What was this power idea of Claude's? I gathered from the paper that it was something quite definite in his mind.'

'Don't know,' Strumer said, 'except this. When he was here last, years ago, he talked a certain amount of that stuff; but I put it down to immaturity then. I suppose now it's got some of the dust and dignity of middle age.'

'What's it all about?'

'Simply, it was an exaggerated form of individualism as the only basis of any co-operative effort. He started, I imagine the idea started in his mind with the failure of love as the substitute for religion.'

'How?'

'The first proposition would be: religion has broken down, either as the motor-force of public or private life; what force it has is restrictive. So there's

ABOUT LEVY

a need to find some new motor-force. Most people try to find it in love (human love and union that is, their widest sense), in the place of love for a God whose interest they can no longer believe is directed towards us.'

'And does that fail too?'

'I don't know that it does. But I remember Claude made this comparison between the individual and a fence set firm in the earth and standing high. A true marriage would be two such fences leant together as a roof, providing shelter beneath it and a greater resistance to pressure from on top or from the sides. Such an arrangement would be more secure than the former, but the height or reach reduced. Actual marriage to-day was seldom such a union, but the willing or unwilling subordination of one party to the other. It was the fence pulled over with weights; or in some cases it was the union of two inferior people against the world, not for it. That is, marriage is usually either a non-social or an anti-social act.'

'The kettle's boiling,' Common said. 'Shall I go to it?'

'No, sit here.' Strumer went out.

He came back with a tea-tray. Putting it down, he said, 'God, it's good to have someone here who's not a half-wit.'

'The solution then is in individual power, either in marriage or out of it?' Common said.

'Yes.'

'But in marriage there must be some other criterion besides power. He must believe in love as a motor-force, as you call it. If it were only power, marriage would be a perpetual attempt to subordinate the partner.'

'It's a question, as they say. By power I take it he means what Aristotle means by ἐνέργεια, if you'll excuse my pedantry; or what Blake meant by "energy is eternal delight." '

'What did Aristotle mean by ἐνέργεια? You must remember that I'm just back from darkest Africa, where power has the definite meaning of control of one man by another.'

'It would in Africa. Certainly control is part of the meaning of energy. It's both the force of living and the ability to direct the force in yourself and others. Power implies direction. Its importance is primary. Everybody must have direction. Love is certainly the basis of marriage; but it must be the union of direction; the strengthening of purposes and not their deflection.'

He began to pour out tea, but continued talking. 'Not like snails in intercourse, oblivious of the world. Sugar and milk?'

'The idea of two people getting married in order to work in a cause seems to me a distortion of lust.'

'A world of Mr. and Mrs. Sidney Webbs?' Strumer said. 'We could do with more of them. But what Claude was getting at primarily is that the individual has lost his right of individualism because the power has gone out of him and he has no longer any direction.'

Common lit a cigarette. 'I don't know England now; but if it's the same as I left it, it's true that the individual doesn't seem to have much sense of direction. But I think that Claude's theory has got implications which you don't admit. It's directly opposed to love. Social direction must be forgotten in love or marriage will become beastly.'

'I'm married. I'm Claude's exponent, not his disciple. I agree there's a fundamental contradiction in his attitude; one which I thought appeared at its nastiest during the trial, when he spoke of his proposal to the girl as though he was making a sacrifice. Besides, his attitude can't be generalised.'

'Did he say that? I didn't see that.'

'What troubles me is this. I can imagine myself talking as Levy talked; but with me, and I believe with most other people, half of my theories of that sort are fraud and the other half self-justification. I can imagine myself giving out that I had proposed to a pretty girl for her own good after I'd been turned down by her. I can even imagine myself believing it. But I cannot imagine myself doing it.'

'I quite agree. He must either be a saint or a eunuch.'

'I prefer to think he was neither.'

Strumer paused and lit a cigarette.

'What do you think then?'

'I think he was an ordinary man, but that owing

to some shock, probably some sexual repulse soon after he left school, a disjunction arose between his physical and mental life. His mind tyrannised over his body; a popular tyranny, mind you, in which the tyrant placated his subjects by decreeing their will as his own, sometimes. He sublimated his desire by quasi-avuncular relationships of the type he seems to have had with Edith Mason. Secretly he was in love with her, but he concealed it from himself even, calling it a disinterested desire for her good. He couldn't, however, stand a rival in Christopher Hall, whom he had in his power owing to this unfortunate confession. There were three steps. First he tried to dissuade Hall from the marriage on medical and other grounds; that failing, he proposed to the girl himself. By that stage he was becoming distraught.—The girl, you remember, mentioned the strangeness of his manner.—And, finally, when she turned him down, he went round to threaten Hall. I believe that he quite sincerely had those pellets made up with the intention of poisoning a dog, and had too many made without consciously knowing why. I believe that the opportunity happening to arise, without knowing what he did, he poisoned Hall, and, as soon as he had done it, regained his normal senses. That is, the popular tyrant was for the moment deposed and rendered helpless, though he has now been recalled.'

Common smiled and said, 'Very ingenious. I don't know enough about abnormal psychology to

ABOUT LEVY

know whether it's possible or not. But it seems a little *too* ingenious. The first part may be true; but the total amnesia you suggest is surely unlikely; especially as he seems to have given almost immediately afterwards a coherent explanation from which he hasn't budged since. Surely the thing was premeditated or nothing.'

'It's just a theory of mine, of course,' Strumer said.

'Half self-justification and half fraud?'

36. Then somebody said, 'Jesus Christ couldn't have existed if we judge from ourselves.'

Freeman cleared his throat and said, 'I quite agree, Mr. Jenkins, with your religious views . . . but this is a court of law. We're discussing Claude Levy, not Jesus Christ.'

'I'm sorry I spoke,' Mr. Jenkins said.

'But the question we're trying to decide, though we keep on wandering from the point, is whether the accused's evidence is to be believed or not,' Miss Ffrancis said. 'Isn't that right, Mr. Foreman?'

'That's perfectly correct.'

'Well, don't you think the psychological element enters into it also?'

'You mean?'

'That not only does the accused's account of the crime seem impossible . . .'

'Improbable,' Mould said.

'Improbable then, if not impossible; but also his account of himself and his motives seems to me to be almost incredible. Take the facts. Hall

ABOUT LEVY

proposes to Miss Mason. The doctor tries to dissuade her, partly, he tells her, because Hall is a rotter . . .'

'Which was true,' Mould said.

'Perfectly true, Mr. Mould,' Freeman said, 'but nothing to do with the case, which is whether the accused killed the deceased. Please do not interrupt Miss Ffrancis. Will you continue, Miss Ffrancis?'

'Partly because Hall was a rotter and partly because he wanted to marry her himself. Miss Mason refused him and accepted Hall. Levy admits he was prepared to stop the marriage at all costs. Then Hall is poisoned and Levy discovered in the room.'

'If you gave the facts to anyone, and said, "These facts are connected; what is the connection?" They could tell you immediately. But the accused says in effect, "No. In order to understand this case you must forget all you know about human nature. I am a creature entirely different from you all. When I propose to a beautiful girl, I do not love her. I am prepared to sacrifice myself for her benefit. When I try to dissuade the man she has chosen in preference to me, I am doing it for his good and hers, but not my own. When this girl conceives the estimable, if romantic, idea of saving this young man from himself, I alone realise that she is having a bad and not a good influence over him. To me the laws of human nature do not apply, though I recognise that they do to others; with the exception of my victim to whom the laws of intoxication do not apply." '

ABOUT LEVY

She finished speaking. All had listened to her. Two nodded when she had ended, and smiled.

'Miss Ffrancis has put more forcefully than I could what I myself feel to be correct,' Freeman said. 'We are men and women of the world here: not children to be taken in by a fairy-tale. Myself, I sympathise with the accused quite a deal. I see him a passionate man, whose feelings ran away with him. I agree with both our friends here that Hall was not a man that any of us would have liked to meet, or respected if we had met him. But that is not the point. We have talked for some time, and I think we have discussed the whole thing thoroughly. It is time I put the question to you: was the accused guilty of the murder of Christopher Hall?'

All except Chappell and Mould held up their hands.

Chappell held up his hand.

Mould held up his hand.

37. The cars began to speed out all ways from the street and the circus, slowing only at corners to throw out bundles to the men and boys there. These grabbed them and tore the string off, crying '*Star* and *News* and *Standard* Special.' Then they took out the posters and ran shouting down the streets, knocking them out each step with their knees. 'Levy Sensational Developments; Levy Murder Trial.' And stopped to sell, the eyes roving always for the next buyer. Men and women bought, walking along streets or turning into the Tube; and they came out of shops to buy; and heads looked out of windows high in blocks of flats as the boys called '*Star* and *Standard, News* and *Standard* Special.'

The cars went on, threading the traffic, driven on brakes constantly; narrow and red, creeping to the front in traffic blocks and slipping round corners when the light-signal went yellow.

They stopped at railways and unloaded packet

ABOUT LEVY

after packet, and these were flung into the vans, and the trains started and took them into the outer belt of London, to Blackheath and Epsom and Berkhamstead; and there too the boys went crying, 'Murder Trial Sensation,' from the station up the High Street and through the towns.

Mr. (Tommy) Bright bought his paper at Blackfriars Station, and read it before crossing the road. 'Edith's Collapse in Tea Shop. Cab-driver's story. Edith says, "I cannot speak." "There were tears in her eyes," said Mr. Albert Smith, the driver of the taxi which was summoned by our special correspondent to take Edith to her home. Before she got out she powdered her face and made up her lips so that no one should see that she had been crying, a great example of the pluck of modern girlhood.' It was all there.

He went over to the office.

The liftman smiled. Then he nodded his head in the direction of the wall. Bright's photograph was up on the walls again.

'Fine weather ahead, sir.'

'Yes, Tom; thirsty too, I expect.' He put a shilling in his hand.

Tom shut the gates. The lift leapt up.

They nodded to him as he walked out of the lift.

'*He* wants to see you.'

He passed across and knocked and opened a door.

ABOUT LEVY

'Hallo, Bright.'

'Got my stuff, I see.'

'It is the dope. Smart work, Bright.'

'I was in luck.'

'You needed it.'

'Came at the right moment, didn't it?'

'It sure did, as the Yanks say.'

'Anything you're wanting particularly?'

'No, Bright; keep the way you're going and you'll do. But mind, you've got the goods once, but don't think that's the whole vanload.'

'No, sir.'

'Prompt and regular delivery, see?'

'Yes.'

Bright turned to go.

'By the way, Bright, ever done any special feature stuff?'

'No, sir.'

'Well, try your hand. I'll give you a line. Go to the Battersea Dogs' Home. That'll give you a snappy par. Let your imagination go a bit.'

'Snappy's the word,' Bright said. 'Do my best.'

'You'll do it, Bright. Sure you will. I believe in you. Always have.'

They shook hands.

'Then you might try Theosophy. Get a shot of one of those niggers togged up for a ceremonial. Or there's the toy-sellers on the steps of St. Martin's. There's a human story there. Seen 'em?'

'Yes,' Bright said.

ABOUT LEVY

'Got some cute things. Bought one of those wooden things: swing a wooden knob round on the end of a bit of string and the hens peck. The kids loved it. Well, so long. You try them.'

'I will,' Bright said, 'so long.'

38. Miriam went down the stairs.

Irène called after her, 'Are you sure I can't get you a taxi? You'll be all right?'

'I'll be all right. Good-bye.'

Irène called down, 'Come and see me to-morrow.'

Miriam went on down. The staircase seemed to be swinging like a boat.

'Come if you can, then,' Irène called. 'Don't, if you don't want to. Good-bye.'

Miriam waved and said, 'Good-bye.' She caught hold of the banisters, closing her eyes against the swinging.

She was in the hall, and suddenly the noise, '*Star, News* and *Standard*,' suddenly, 'Levy Murder Sensation,' filled the hall. She saw a boy go past, shouting. She opened her mouth to call him. Then she did not call, but sat on the horse-hair sofa, trembling.

The noise of his voice rose and dropped, rose and died. Silence was laid across the noise of cars.

A man and woman were walking up the steps.

ABOUT LEVY

She got up and passed them at the door. They did not look at her. As they were coming towards her, the man said, 'Of course, she always took life very seriously.' As they went away the woman said, 'She had lovely teeth.'

She was on the pavement and walking down to the station. She bought a paper at the Kiosk. 'Edith's Collapse in Tea Shop.' She looked it through in the lift. She looked at the Stop Press News: 'Surrey, 61 for 2, Yorkshire all out, 302; 2.30, Billy Boy, Heart's Desire, Straight Die.' She closed the paper. They filed out into the tunnel and went down the stairs.

Go to Ken Wood by Underground.

She got into the carriage and sat down. Three women came in talking. The man opposite was reading about 'Edith's Collapse in London Tea Shop.' Then he looked at the Stop Press News.

The train jerked and started.

She looked at the paper—at the photograph of Edith Mason. She screened herself round, but could not read it. Several times she glanced it through, but could see no mention of a verdict. The jury had retired, were still sitting. She could not read the summing up.

She got out at Strand Station and went up into Trafalgar Square.

Men were sleeping in the sun and children feeding pigeons. One man was asleep with his head in arm rested on a bowl of a fountain. The

ABOUT LEVY

buses and lorries and cars wound in and round and out of the square.

She walked up and down until she felt tired. Then she went to a seat and sat down. Her closed eyelids were running red against the sun.

A man next her said, 'It's going to rain to-day.'

She looked up at the sky and said, 'Yes, it may.'

'There'll be thunder, too,' he said.

She felt exhausted.

'May I borrow your paper, miss?' he said.

She gave it to him.

'Funny case, this Levy business,' the man said.

She closed her eyes, pretending to be so tired.

'No verdict yet?' the man went on. 'Still, I don't think there's much doubt what it'll be.'

She listened. But the man said nothing.

Then she opened her eyes, and said, 'What will it be?'

'Guilty,' the man said. 'I've not got the slightest doubt about it in my own mind.'

'I see,' she said, and lay still, her head caught at the neck by the back edge of the seat.

' "Billy Boy," ' the man said. 'Blind me, a fellow tipped me that last night. "Watch Billy Boy," he said, "for the two-thirty or the three-thirty. 'E's entered for both, and the one 'e runs in 'e'll win." Thirty-three-to-one, starting price! My God! that's my luck.'

She saw a red van stop at the corner of the Strand and boys stopping when it went on, and then

ABOUT LEVY

breaking away, one coming towards her. Each moment he was stopped. She got up and hurried towards him.

'Levy Murder Verdict, miss,' the boy said.

She took the paper.

LEVY GUILTY.

She felt sick and as if she might fall. She saw the boy's face look up at her in astonishment. Then people were round him buying.

39. Edith still watched the street with her eyes, but images of her confession to perjury followed each other through her brain. This time that all the presses of Fleet and Tudor Streets, and Odhams lodged in Longacre, should start and roll out her deliberate lies along a page. This would save Claude certainly; for it would swing a pendulum to him that would have been still, if she had spoken the truth at first. Herself would rescue the man she had nearly convicted, and turn despised heroine who had been admired villainess.

The thought sent blood pumping, so that her whole body seemed beating heart. She flushed, and her breathing came hard.

Those would blame her who had idly admired before. But those, Claude among them, who had seen malice under glib answer, would be turned to praise.

She watched the street.

A boy came past the house, '*Star*, *News* and *Standard*' and shouted up at her, 'Levy Murder

Sensation,' seeing her staring out. When she did not answer, he went on crying, 'Lunch Time Scores' and 'Levy Sensation.'

Her chin was on her hand, propped from the knee. She tightened the tension with fingers along bone and jaw firm closed, so that she was fixed into determination.

She remained thus until her muscles ached. Then she bent head, hooding eyes with hands. She closed her eyes, and her mind was rapt into still darkness.

When she opened them she saw gaps in the mesh of fingers, and the small finger bent away inwards from the rest, and the window-sill between the gaps.

You make him evil, Claude said, because that's how you like him. I said, if you knew how sad it makes me to see him drunk and debased, you wouldn't say that. He said, I know it makes you feel sad, but that's what you like to feel. You want to pity not to love him. Don't, I said, feeling all dizzy. He said, It's been worse since you began saving him. He sees you like him better when he's sotted than sober, and he plays up to it. I couldn't go, remember, though he didn't do anything to stop me; I felt so limp. He said, Do you remember when you told me how you had to take him home at nine o'clock one evening, he was so drunk: and you went up and undressed him? Then he was so tight he couldn't stand up, yet his skin was soft and fresh like a child's. I got him into bed somehow, I never knew how, and the clothes over him. He said, Come to bed. And I stood there waiting till he should fall asleep. Then he

ABOUT LEVY

sat up and said, Kiss me. I said, You're drunk again, Chris. I shall never see you again. He said, Let me kiss your hand. I put my hand down and he took it and covered it with kisses. I passed my hand through his hair; and so he fell asleep, his head against my hand. I said, You're jealous of him, Claude. That's what it is. When I'd said that, I could get up, and left him.

She shivered, and pain crossed her face. Then she got up and pulled a dressing-case from beneath the bed and packed it. She put her cheque-book in her bag and went to the door and listened. She took her dressing-case from the bed and unlocked the door, listened again and then went tiptoe down the stairs. She opened the front door, which creaked, and when she swung it to, the latch made a snapping entering the catch.

She was outside. She ran down the steps. The sky was black over London. Her feet were all hurry to the Underground.

She took a ticket to Waterloo and went below. Caught a train immediately. Everything went fast and in her favour. She kept humming a tune.

She went along the tunnel up into the great station. People were threading to the platforms under the darkness. A porter took her bag.

'Where for, miss?'

She went and looked at the indicator. Then she said, 'Dorchester.'

'Got a ticket?'

'No, I must get one.' She turned.

ABOUT LEVY

'Shall I get you a paper, miss?'

'No, I don't want one.'

The lightning splashed down and drenched the building.

'Dorchester.'

Thunder came after.

'Where?'

'Dorchester.'

She paid the money down and got a ticket.

'You'll have to run,' the porter said.

They got through just before the gates were closed. They were turning down the handles of the carriages. The porter swung open a door. She got in.

'Empty one. Thank you, miss.'

He slammed the door to. The train whistled. Lightning lit him up. The guard whistled. The train began to draw out of the shade of the station. Thunder shivered on the roof. The shade of the station slid along the train.

Then rain struck in. She drew up the window. Drops splayed and sputtered on the dusty glass.

40. 'THE O.R.'s look as though they'll win,' Strumer said.

'Yes, the school's got a weak team this year, hasn't it?'

'I've never known a year in which it hadn't. Last year at this place is always fair, and next year is always going to be "definitely good."'

'It shows a healthy spirit of optimism,' Common said.

'Yes. It's the only thing that has kept one stone on another.'

They stopped in the shadow of the school buildings and got out.

'When's the News Bulletin?'

'Six,' Strumer said.

'Quite soon then.'

Most of the parents had gone; a knot, whose sons were playing, and Bubb and Hill watched the game still from the pavilion.

'Thirty-two runs to make in as many minutes,' Father Hill said. 'The school's playing for a draw.'

'It's been a very wonderful day, really,' Bubb said.

ABOUT LEVY

'We couldn't have had better weather if we had ordered it.'

'I'm not a devout man, Bubb,' Strumer said, 'but I've always prayed for fine weather on Speech Day since I ceased to be a house-master. Before that I used to pray for rain, because it kept parents away and sent those home early who came at all. To-day the Almighty has seen fit to listen to my prayer, and I think we might in all reverence pass a hearty vote of thanks.'

'There's many a true word spoken in jest, Strumer.'

'And many a false one spoken in earnest, Bubb.'

'Can't you watch the game?' Hill said.

'Is anyone listening in?' Common said.

'Surrey was sixty-two for two at lunch-time,' Hill said; 'you probably heard that. They'll have all the scores at the lodge.'

'Father Beasley is listening in,' Bubb said, 'if you want to hear the result of the trial.'

'Do you think I can go up?'

'I'm sure you can. Have you met him?'

'No.'

'I'll take you up.'

They walked over to the school.

'I'm sorry about Strumer,' Common said.

'It's his game; he calls it priest-baiting.'

'It's rather offensive.'

'He thinks he's helping Galileo and Servetus to get a little of their own back. It doesn't worry me.'

ABOUT LEVY

They walked on. Then Bubb said, 'I assure you I'm very grieved about Claude Levy.'

'It was a shock to me.'

'It was a shock to all of us. Though perhaps not to all of us as great a shock as it was to you.'

'Why?'

'There are helps in life, aids which the Church gives. We don't say there is only one way to salvation; but we know one certain way. And when anyone repudiates that help, as he did even at school, we are not surprised at misfortune overtaking them!'

'Even perhaps a bit pleased?'

'We are never pleased to see the decline of any spirit through sin, but we are not as surprised by it as you are. It is a spiritual law.'

'I see the chaplain's moved,' Common said.

'Yes, the old room was very draughty. You can remember that, I expect. This is his new room.'

They knocked and went in. Beasley was sprawled along an old sofa.

'This is Common, an O.R., Father Beasley,' Bubb said. 'He wants to hear the news.'

'Woe is me, as the prophet saith,' Beasley said. 'I turned it off when they got to the cricket scores. What do you want to know?'

'The result of the Levy trial.'

'Condemned to death.'

'I see,' Common said. 'Thank you.'

Bubb followed him out like his shadow and took his arm and said, 'I'm awfully sorry.'

ABOUT LEVY

'Of course you are,' Common said. 'You're paid to be sorry.'

'One of the things I'm paid to know is that a woman shows grief by weeping, a man by being rude.'

'I'm sorry I was rude. I want to be alone now.'

Bubb went back to the chaplain's room. Common walked slowly downstairs. He did not think of Claude, but of the silence that covered the negroes as the man lay in the dust, and their suddenly shouting, and how clean he felt. He looked out at the memory as if he were standing deep in a cave and saw it happen in a clear sunshine.

Then he said, 'It's not the same case at all.'

A boy who was passing looked hard at him, and turned to see who talked to himself.

Strumer was in the lodge. The match was over.

'Have you heard?'

'Yes, I've heard,' Strumer said.

'Well? What do you think of it?'

'He's been unlucky.'

'I feel he can't have done it.'

'That's not evidence.'

'I know it's not. But it's impossible that he should have done it. After all, you and I know him.'

'Do we? You haven't seen him for what—thirteen years? I for nine. What did we really know of him then? He wasn't a murderer then; because he hadn't committed a murder. I never know whether a man's a murderer. You can't tell by his face, pardoning

ABOUT LEVY

Lombroso, or even by his finger-prints. Experts have got to make a living. I just don't know. All I say is that he's been unlucky. Everybody is, who is condemned to death.'

'There's sure to be an appeal.'

'Yes, but since it was set up the Court of Criminal Appeal has only once reversed the verdict in a murder trial.'

Hill came up and said, 'It's terrible, isn't it? Really terrible.'

'Yes,' Common said.

'And it doesn't do the school any good,' Hill said. 'The headmaster is very sad.'

'We might lodge an appeal to the Home Secretary,' Strumer said, 'representing that while we fully recognise that Claude Levy is guilty, it would be bad for the school that he should be hanged by the neck until he was dead, but that his sentence should be commuted to penal servitude for life.'

'Sometimes your wilful misunderstanding makes me very angry, Strumer. The effect on the school is an aspect of the case we have got to admit.' Then he turned to Common. 'I'm a busy man, Diddlums, but if you are ever in my direction look me up. There's not a finer or more loyal set of people in the country than my parishioners, though they live in the worst slums I know. You could come down to the club and help with the boxing. I know you'd like that.'

'If I can, I will,' Common said.

ABOUT LEVY

Hill held out his hand and squeezed Common's. 'Good-bye, Diddlums.'

Common returned the pressure, and rubbed the bones together so hard that Hill said, 'You're hurting me.'

'I'm sorry,' Common said. 'In Africa, we sometimes find snakes in the veldt. We have to catch hold of them like that to prevent their hurting us.'

41. 'SURREY all out, 274. Play ceased owing to rain.'

'Turn that damn thing off,' Mason said.

'What's that?' the girl said.

'Do you mind, miss?'

'That's better.'

The girl went out.

They looked up at the great fretwork square slung in the corner of the room.

'Lancashire two hun—' the sound died with noise like a tapped drum.

'Guilty,' Mrs. Failey said.

The girl's head said, 'Is that all right?'

'Yes, thanks, miss. And two more of the same.'

'You hevn't trayed one of ah Gaytecresher Cocktails yet. Only sixpence. They're quayte splendid.'

Mason looked at Mrs. Failey.

'I'm sticking to my usual, Charles. If that name means anything, it's the cocktail you give to gatecrashers, and I know what that's like.'

'I think another time,' Mason said. 'Two more pink gins for now.'

ABOUT LEVY

When the girl went out, he said, 'I never expected anything else. Not really. It gave me a shock, I admit; but the sort of shock you get when what you always say is going to happen really does happen.'

'Yet you didn't seem really certain.'

'I was trying to put his case to you. That's what it was.'

'And you think he was guilty?'

'Here's to your lively eyes,' he said; 'I might say *deadly* eyes.'

'Coupled with Droitwich brine,' she said.

'Yes, huhuh,' he said, 'huh-huh.' His laugh was like a Lewis gun. 'But what I mean is this; there are those who say, "Be tried by a jury, that's a toss up." Some say it, Levy said it himself. But I say "No." It's not the jury that tries you. They're just there for the form of the thing. The judge is the man. They don't know what to think. But the judge tells them.'

'That's true, Charles.'

'He knows, does the judge. What he says goes with me; and would go, too, even if I didn't know what I do know of Mr. Levy.'

'What do you know?'

'I know this; another pink gin; he's left the beaten track. He might say he was normal.'

'I'll have another, Charles. You won't leave me behind. And what does that mean?'

'It means this; that it's ideas and things like that make a man mad and lead to murder and crime of all

ABOUT LEVY

sorts. And we, who take things as they come, the pleasure with the pain, the bitters with the gin, we get the most out of life, we put the most in it. Isn't that so?'

'It is, Charles; it certainly is.'

Oh, her eyes, her eyes, set in that blank face alike, are like, like two of something very marvellous.

'Happy days,' she said.

'Happy nights, huhuh,' he laughed, 'huhuhuh.'

42. SHE crossed over to Lyons', went in among the crowded tables, where those were sitting who had been to matinées, programmes laid with bags beside the ices. Sat at a little table for two by a pillar.

At the next table a man said, 'I wonder if the verdict has been given yet?'

'She's got a paper, ask her,' a woman said.

'We'll find out soon enough.'

'You can easily ask her.'

That tipster with a turban passed, his black head and many-coloured shoulders above the others. He had just married, another feather in his turban.

'What will you have, miss?' The girl looked down at her. 'What'll you have?'

'Something cold.'

'Ices, fruit sundaes, paych-melba, iced lemonade, iced coffee.'

'Iced coffee.'

'I'll go out and get a paper, if you're really so keen on knowing,' the man said.

ABOUT LEVY

'No, that would be silly.'

'Have a cigarette?' he said.

'No,' she said. 'I believe you're afraid of asking.'

'It's not a question of "afraid," but of common politeness.'

'If you're afraid, I'll ask her.'

He was drawing his cigarette; then he said, 'Right.'

'Excuse me.'

Miriam did not turn, till the woman touched her arm.

'Does it give the verdict in your paper?'

'It says here that he's guilty.'

'Thank you so much,' the woman said; 'it's very kind of you. I knew you wouldn't mind.'

She sat looking at the words, LEVY GUILTY. Her iced coffee was on the table. The word GUILTY looked wrong; more and more wrong, the u and the I, the more she looked. She did not understand how the six letters could make that word.

She sipped the coffee, of which the cold stung her palate.

Am I mad? He said the verdict was obvious, who took my paper. Claude was my rock, who has crumbled in my hand to powder. If he is guilty and could do this, then all round are guilty. Thieves and adulterers are at these tables. That parson may be incestuous. Even myself may have done crime fouler than imagination, if he this. And yet, perhaps; the solid rock is crushed to powder. The silver cord is loosed; the golden bowl is broken; the pitcher is broken at the fountain and the wheel broken at the cistern.

She took the bill from the table and went to the cashier and paid it. Then she went through the door and stood in the porch. People were hurrying past, talking over their shoulders, and running for buses, and turning in past her for tea. All moved; only she was still. Then she stepped into the stream and was borne away.

The sky was slate black. Rock-like clouds hid the sun. But the air was hot. A man looked up and said 'thunder.'

She turned out of the stream into a back street. There were few people, but what there were hurried. She was walking slowly with eyes fixed on the ground.

'We need rain,' a man said. 'It'll cool the place down and make things cleaner.'

A cool wind blew fast, whipped dust and shook the sun-blinds. Hats were off, ran, spun, and bowled down streets and over roads and under cars. A loose tarpaulin leapt and struck the drayman who tried to fix it. A rack of newspapers was blown from its hook into the gutter and lay at her feet. A dog chased a bicycle past her, barking and leaping at the circling shoes and pedals. Her skirt was thrown out and between her legs.

The air was calm. Lightning split a dark cloud and jumped at her eyes. A sooted wall was licked with yellow. She heard a motor-horn. Then fell down thunder and spread out on the city like débris

ABOUT LEVY

of an avalanche. A rainball hit and broke warm on her lips. She felt others strike through her dress to the skin of her shoulders, fastening the stuff to her body; and this was cold. She looked for shelter—for rain burst itself round her on the dry stones—and went to a portico, up steps.

She stood looking at the rain, which washed down the road and pavement and gathered into a stream, covered with a film of dust that broke and turned on itself and joined.

A taxi splashed down the street.

Lightning again flashed along the street and the bowls of thunder tumbled.

She turned to the building from the cold air. It was a church. She stood at the entrance. Mass, 7.30; 8.30, Sundays; 7.30, week-days. She opened the door, held it open, and then went in.

The rain rattled on the roof like hens pecking on a tray. There was a smell of incense. It was dark inside, but even without silence it was quiet, with a quietness of abstraction. The high altar was hidden away in shadow. She stood looking at it in the space before the seats began. Her lips said, 'Shĕmá Yisráêl Ádhonai Elohênu Ádhonai Echâdh.' She heard her voice saying it again and again monotonously. 'Hear Israel, the Lord is our God, the Lord is one. Shĕmá Yisráêl Ádhonai Elohênu Ádhonai Echâdh.' Her body rocked from side to side.

The lightning seemed to come from all the building, but especially from the window at the east end, and fell on her. The shekinah, the shining presence of the Lord God. The thunder filled each rumbling corner. The Lord God's voice of Hosts was in it.

She was very small. Her spirit was taken back into the god of her race, so that she rocked unconscious, the Shĕma still on her lips. There was no passage of time; nor had Claude existed.

The church was transfigured again with lightning, and again, and shaken with thunder, until the clouds fell in the last shower and the evening sun shone from the clear sky.

Then she turned round and opened the door and went into the steaming street.

43.   The nurse said, 'I've brought you the paper, medem.' She had folded it on the way so that the head-line was turned in. 'I thought you would like to see it.'

Ruth took the paper from her, but did not open it.

'Would you like me to take the children to the nursery?'

She was reading *The Happy Prince* to them.

They said, 'Finish the story; finish the story!'

'It's all right, thank you, nurse.'

They were sitting on the floor resting against her legs and the sofa. The paper was on the cushion beside her. She went on reading the story, which she loved because the language was so rich and brighter than life. But her attention was distracted towards the folded paper at her side. Her voice was not wholly in, nor eyes on, what she read. It was flat champagne, the waiters' drink after the guests are gone. Even when she pulled herself back, to round and fill the words, they grew only distended. John noticed it: his head lay back against her thigh when he was listening; now it was turned towards the clasp of his shoe with which his fingers played.

She looked at the paper, which was opening to its former crease. She could not see yet what the head-line was. She saw, 'In summing up, Mr. Justice Starr . . .' They looked up; she had lost her place.

'Go on,' Hugh said.

She found the place and went on reading.

After a short time she stirred. The cushion moved. The paper was unfolding. She went on reading in a voice which varied in tone as she tried to put expression into what she read, but which had no relation to the words.

Even to see the words and then speak them out was an act which taxed the whole mind. Then she stopped and said to John, 'Fetch me a cigarette, John, darling. They're in that silver box over there.'

John got up and fetched the box.

She looked down at the paper: LEVY GUILTY; turned the paper over and was waiting for him.

She took a cigarette and he lit it for her, and she rested until he came back and sat down against her leg again. Then she began to read.

Now her mind filled the words flush. She was all in all of them, and behind them. The words were a gorgeous creed. She threw away her cigarette and gave herself into reading; and they two were gathered into the force and glory of the words. She

ABOUT LEVY

forgot everything, even her sons at her sides, though they rose with her. Then the palace stood in over-clustered luxury against the world's wind and the mirrors gave back their cheating image and the prince walked through the rooms.

The story was over. They were left, she and the two, each in a perplexity.

They got up and kissed her as she bent down, and Hugh climbed on her knee and hung from her neck. John sat on the sofa and, jogging up and down, said 'Trains,' and pretended to fall asleep against her, which was the next step.

'Go to nurse, now,' she said.

Hugh said, 'No.' But John said, 'Come on, we're going to nurse.' She jumped Hugh down and they went off.

She took the paper and went to her room. She shut and locked the door and opened the paper.

The air came in cool through the window after the storm. The rain still dripped from leaf to leaf to the ground.

She read through nearly all that it said and again the black head-line. A breeze shook down the curtains. She went over to the table by the window where the bowl was, and touched its rim with her fingers. It was quiet and cool.

Feeling her fingers as very delicate, she held the bowl up in them as if they were a stand, above her eyes, so that it stood against the light of the window and the sky at which she looked. The bowl trembled

ABOUT LEVY

on her finger-tips. She did not know, then, whether it slipped; or whether she let it drop.

Bits of it lay on their backs on the floor. Small wedges splintered beneath the table. The paint of the boards was broken where it fell and the wood dented. A large piece, almost a third, was big enough to be a thing in itself; it did not seem a 'bit.' She set her foot on it and pressed with her weight. It snapped and lay flat.

She stared at the mess. Then she unlocked the door and rang the bell. The maid came in.

'Can you get a brush and dustpan, Mary, and sweep up this mess.'

'I thought I heard something fall,' the maid said. 'But I never thought it'd be your lovely vase, which you were so fond of.'

'See that none of the little sharp bits are lying about, because the children might hurt themselves on them.'

'I will indeed, madam. I liked it best of anything in this house, if you'll excuse me.'

'It was a pretty thing,' Ruth said.

44.   'Did you see 'im?'
'See who?'
'The boy,' Sankey said.
'Who d'yer mean?'
'The youngster I sent back.'
'Where is 'e?'
'Inside. 'E got in.'
'Aw, can it.'
'I saw 'im inside,' Sankey said, 'just before the gates shut. He waved to me.'
'Hell, what's it matter?'
'Oh, it doesn't matter. I never said it did matter, did I?'
'Then what yer jawing about?'
'I'm not jawing about anything.'
'Right, then stop jawing about it.'
They walked up the alley among the others and turned left.
The man said, 'Hell.'
'You know what it is?' Sankey said.
'Know what what is?'

ABOUT LEVY

'We're too old. The young ones are getting in. That's what it is.'

'Damn me, if I'm too old,' the man said. 'I can do that work as well as anyone. So can you. You know you can. I can lift as much. You talk of being too old. There's too many of us, that's what it is.'

'It's the same thing in the end,' Sankey said, 'being too many or too old. We go and the young ones come in.'

'That's it. There's too many of us wants a job.'

'I met a man said there's work up on the Clyde,' Sankey said.

They turned up right away from the river.

'What d'yer say to you an' me goin' up to see?' Sankey said.

'I'm married. That's what I say.'

'I know you're married,' Sankey said.

'What is it, anyway?'

'Breaking up ships.'

'Got a Woodbine, pal?'

Sankey gave him one and took one himself. They lit up.

'What about it, eh?'

'I'm sticking where I am,' the man said. 'I'm married.'

'You won't get a bloody job down here.'

'Yer won't get one up there neither.'

They came to 'The Blue Posts.'

'What about one?' Sankey said.

ABOUT LEVY

'I'm broke,' the man said.

'That's all right, pal.'

'I don't like to.'

'Come on,' Sankey said.

They went in. Sankey stood and rapped the bar with a coin. The barman came out.

'Two ales.'

He drew two ales and set them on the counter.

'I'm fed up with bumming around here,' Sankey said. 'It's a job I want.'

'Here's to it.' The man raised his glass and stretched his chin out to it.

'Seen the paper?' the barman said.

'Here's to it,' Sankey said.

'Who won the two-thirty?'

'Billy Boy; then it was . . . let me see'—he picked up the paper—"Eart's Desire, and Straight Die third.'

'Billy Boy!' the man said. 'What did it start at?'

'Thirty-three to one.'

'Shake me hand, pal. That's twenties I got. Bill don't give any more. But it's drinks on me anyway.'

The barman drew himself one and one for each of them.

'Seen about Levy?'

'What've they done about that?' Sankey said.

'Guilty.'

'What are they doin' with 'im?'

'Hanging, of course.'

'Thought as much.'

ABOUT LEVY

'What'd you expect 'em to do. Fall on 'is neck and kiss 'im?'

'He was a man,' Sankey said. 'He's got power, and that's what they're afraid of.'

'Didn't he do it?'

'Of course 'e did it, and so 'e ought. That's what I like about 'im. What was Christopher 'All? A young one trying to get his place. That's all 'e was. I know. I've seen 'em.'

'But they'd got to hang 'im, if he was guilty,' the barman said.

"Aw, I'm sick of hanging around here, waiting for something to turn up.'

'I'll come with you,' the man said.

'What about the wife and kids?'

' "I'm comin' with you," I said. That's what about the wife and kids.'

'What about these drinks?' the barman said.

'Just goin' round to collect the cash,' the man said. 'I'll be back rightaway.'

'That's not good enough,' the barman said.

'It's got to be,' the man said. 'Come on, pal.'

They went outside.

The man said, 'The Clyde, you said?'

'There's work up there,' Sankey said.

'Yes, I know,' the man said. 'I'll meet you at your place in half an hour's time.'

'Right,' Sankey said. 'I'm fed up with this burg. What about that quid?'

'We won't wait for that,' the man said.